Bedford Square 5

New Writing from the
Royal Holloway Creative Writing Programme

Foreword by Andrew Motion

Published by Ward Wood Publishing
6 The Drive
Golders Green
London NW11 9SR
www.wardwoodpublishing.co.uk

Foreword © Andrew Motion 2011.

Copyright of individual work remains with each author.
The moral right of authors has been asserted.
Full details of copyright holders can be found on page 229.

ISBN 978-1-908742-06-3

British Library Cataloguing in Publication Data. A CIP record for this book can be obtained from the British Library.

All rights reserved. No part of this publication may be reproduced, stored in a retrieval system, or transmitted in any form or by any means, electronic, mechanical, photocopying, recording or otherwise without the prior written permission of the publishers. This book may not be lent, hired out, resold or otherwise disposed of by way of trade in any form of binding or cover other than that in which it is published, without the prior consent of the publishers.

Designed and typeset in Garamond and Palatino Linotype by Ward Wood Publishing.

Cover Design by Mike Fortune-Wood
Artwork: Pressed Old Handmade Rice Paper by Tombaky
and Abstract Painting by R. Gino Santa Maria
Both supplied by Dreamstime.com

Printed and bound in Great Britain by
Imprint Digital, Seychelles Farm,
Upton Pyne, Exeter EX5 5HY.

The views expressed in this book are those of the individual authors, and do not necessarily represent the opinions of the editors or publishers. All the characters in this book are fictitious and any resemblance to actual persons (living or dead) or to institutions is purely coincidental.

Bedford Square 5

Contents

Foreword by Andrew Motion   7

April Estrada	Selected Poems	9
Nora Gombos	Pitchpoled	15
Hilary Standing	The Inheritance Powder	19
Diriye Osman	Ndambi	24
Kayo Chingonyi	Selected Poems	29
Eamonn Doran	*Eau de Vie*	35
Sally Skinner	Man, Walking	40
Cecilia Ekback	Wolf Winter	45
Helen Adie	Selected Poems	50
Georgina Wolfe	*Étienne*	55
J.K. Benecke	What Jack Did	59
Rebecca Mackenzie	Aboard a White Ship	65
James Trevelyan	Selected Poems	70
L.E. Peters	The Chinese Room	76
Timothy Allsop	Edify	81
Annabel Banks	Faringdon Park	86
Christian Ward	Selected Poems	92
David Gill	The Lives of the Saints	98
William Fowler	Time Death	103
Thomas Ogier	Disappear Here	107
Nigel Pollitt	Selected Poems	114
Lauren Trimble	Southwest Twizzle	120
Rosie Miller	The Tulip	125
Jenni Fagan	Porcelain Sunflower Seeds	131
Marion Ashton	Selected Poems	136
Carl Newbrook	Abundance	142
Saskia Sarginson	No Long Way Round	147
Kristina Heaney	Ava Gates	152
Rachel Piercey	Selected Poems	157
Katy Tucker	A Darkness in the Bones	163
Mary Chamberlain	The Excursion	168
Anna Kirk	Selected Poems	173
Laura McClelland	The Strawberry Thief	179
Viv Graveson	Silence & Shadows	184
Barney Norris	Longing	190

Lyn Thornton	Selected Poems	194
Rebecca Perl	Keep Your Belief Strong	201
Elizabeth Dawson	Lost and Found	206
Sophie Playle	The City, The Sky, The Others	211
Tracy Horn	Selected Poems	215

About the Authors   219

Alphabetical Listing of Authors   228

Copyright Holders   229

Foreword

Anthologies such as this have a special purpose and pleasure: their intention is to provide a shop-window for writers near the start of their writing lives, and the benefits they give readers have to do with new energy and a general freshness of approach. These are important things – they are beacons that illuminate the future – but in this case the work on show offers more than the pleasures of novelty. It also gives us clear proof of accomplishment, so that as readers we feel both brought forward and steadied. It is an exciting mixture, and appropriately enough is matched by a rich variety of tones and moods and techniques within the work itself. Taken as a whole, it bears witness to an unusual accomplishment.

Andrew Motion

Selected Poems

April Estrada

Waiting for the Train

Eight tiny but strange hungers rage
along the coast of your thoughts. The wind
blows, kissing lips blue. You click
your tongue against bitter coffee,
savouring such tastes, such poisons tainting
the new year. You'd like to eat soil;

earth scenting your breath, shedding
the pretentious mint of toothpaste. Hunger
trembles through fingers, fisting the palm
to white knuckles. The feeling
slips to knees and you consider
running – even in slick-bottomed shoes.

Morning

Chinese people are living in my kitchen. I shuffle
    to the cabinet, pull out a glass.
       I hear the fridge door   pop
open — jangling the jars of jams and dressings —

turn in time to see Li
               halfway out, feet first.
We say good morning
    and he passes me the skimmed
milk. As I fill my glass, the large drawer
       next to the oven shudders.
Slender fingers
        slide
through a small   gap,   gripping the face
of the cabinetry and pushing   away. Lithely
Mae
    unfolds,
her thin legs covered in a silky
material with small smiling fish all over.

                Kicking
the drawer shut, she stretches
              her narrow arms
                     above her head. A shy
smile for me, she turns
     to Li and they begin middle conversations
as though never pausing for eight
       hours of sleep. They jostle

             pots
         and pans
for their breakfast; mine is still undecided.

I listen   to a flow and halt   of language
that is beyond me. Finally I settle
    on oatmeal.

                    Opening the pantry,
I am startled by Shan as she rolls
    her linens into empty canisters.
She grabs all-purpose flour
            and baking soda for the Crullers

she already knows
        Mae and Li are making.

                We dance left,
right,   and pass each other
    in the narrow doorway. I tuck

into the pantry, softly bringing the door
closed after.
        With the can
            of Quaker Oats
        cradled in elbows,
I pleat
    myself
into the small space between
    floor
        and
    shelf.

Line Art

I gathered stray strands of hair from the sink,
pinching them between thumb and fore-
finger, plastering them to the wall, away
from the drain. As I brushed my teeth
I followed the line art my hair made against
the high gloss, white paint.

Figures and faces entwined, as I picked
layered lengths from paddle brush, moistened each
strand to stick against the wall. Gently I molded profiles,
added more to create wind-swept
hair. But fingers are clumsy and thick:
I began using tweezers, a pair in both hands,
holding my breath to keep from disrupting
forms.

I used a simple glue: a mixture
of all purpose flour and water. The natural
dampness of the bathroom kept the fixative
pliable.

In the absence of loose tendrils, I began
plucking them from my scalp; my widow's peak
flat-lined along my forehead. Then there was the matter
of depth – the flat, dark brown of my natural
hair was confused in too many layers. So I searched
out vibrant blondes and redheads on the train
and the Underground, where bodies were pressed
into one another. Ecstatic curls wound around
my fingers easily, and sprang out of the portraits.

Even the silvery/white of aged hair
wove in and out, highlighting the brightest
brights. Quick pinches of coats
was the easiest way of hunting and gathering, though
the lure of golden honey hues led,
on occasion, to the snatching of single
strings from unsuspecting follicles.

Twin Burning

She stitched my phantom twin
with the end of yarn that made
me. My sister was tucked
away into closet, hidden
from greedy hands that would soil,
stain the threads
of our making.

I dreamt one night that I
was in a closet – but
it was bright, orange
and hot. I was burning.
There was no pain when I lifted
fingerless palms before
my eyes as I watched flames
swallow my legs. I screamed
but only cotton stuffing
flowed from my mouth, ripped
stitches dangling around lips.

Life Lines

Rag dolls are pliable,
soft around the edges.
Stick one with a needle
and it will come out the other
side – we do not bleed
red, just fuzzy bits of white
cotton (though now we are often
made with synthetic stuffings).

    My new mother cut her hand
    once. I placed my yarn palm
    to her flesh one, felt the liquid
    warmth seep through.
    The life line of my palm now vibrant,
    crimson. There, she said, now that we
    share blood no one can say
    you are not mine.

Pitchpoled

Nora Gombos

An excerpt from the novel. The scene is a flashback to a summer Greta spent with her grandmother Judith on the island.

When I returned, I discovered some abnormally large shoes parked in the hallway. There were muffled voices coming from the living room. I shed my outer layers, and went in to join them.
 'Hey, Uncle Jack!' I said.
 'Good day, Greta,' he replied, genuinely pleased to see me. Uncle Jack is always genuinely pleased to see everyone. He likes people. I think it's because a lot of the cruelty in the world doesn't filter through to him. Or if it does, it doesn't seem to grab hold. Uncle Jack is what people would refer to as slow. He needs more time to learn and understand things than most people, and often repeated attempts. But what he lacks in intellectual capacity, he more than makes up for in generosity. And feet size. He has the largest feet I have ever seen.
 'New summer shoes?' I asked.
 'Yes,' he beamed proudly.
 'They look different from the last pair,' I teased him.
 'No, they are exactly the same.'
Large feet are a curious trait that afflicts men on my grandfather's side of the family. Like my grandfather, and the generations before him, Uncle Jack has to order tailor-made shoes from a speciality shop in London. He only owns three pairs: one for summer, one for winter and one for special occasions. When he exhausts a pair, he orders a new one in the exact same style.
 'Are you staying for lunch?'
 'No, I have to go home,' he replied. 'Jane is making lunch.'
 Uncle Jack had met his wife Jane at a week-long pottery course in Dorset six years earlier. It was love at first sight, and after a week of making sweet music together, and a lot of wonky ceramic bowls and vases, they got married. When Rose found out, she called Judith and screamed at her for letting it happen. Judith explained that there was nothing she could do, and it was better that he had

someone because she wouldn't always be around. 'I guess that proves there's someone for everyone,' my mother hissed and hung up. After the wedding, Uncle Jack and Jane moved into a house next to my grandmother's, which in that part of the island means a brisk walk. A year later their son Oliver arrived, at which point Judith sat them down to explain the concept of contraception.

'What is she making for lunch?' I asked.

'She is baking a cake.'

'For lunch?' I said, feigning shock.

'Yes,' he said, and seemed very excited about the prospect of having cake for lunch.

'I'm envious.'

'I will save you some. And I will save some for Judith too.'

'Thank you,' my grandmother said. 'That's very nice of you.'

'Did you have a nice walk, Greta?' he asked.

'It was a bit windy,' I said.

'Well, it is a very windy island.'

'Yes, it certainly is. It's the windiest island I've ever been on,' I said, which always seemed to please the locals, as if they'd won a competition. And thus we were caught in yet another conversation about wind. Actually, it was another version of the same conversation, which always revolved around how windy it was. The whole island was obsessed with this topic. No one ever seemed to run out of things to say about wind, as days without any wind were few and far between, and several consecutive windless days would warrant a front-page headline in the local paper. Wind was even the number one cause of contention with residents on the other islands in the archipelago, who also claimed that their islands endured the roughest wind conditions.

Knowing about wind was so important that, at the age of seven, the first summer I spent alone with my grandmother, Uncle Jack sat with me in the hammock outside the house for a whole afternoon and helped me memorise the Beaufort scale from a book. My three favourite wind conditions were:

1. Beaufort 0 – Calm

Uncle Jack's book said that in calm wind condition, the sea looks like a mirror and the air movement is so slight that smoke rises vertically. Although I never experienced Calm on the island, it was how being there made me feel on the inside.

2. Beaufort 3 – Gentle Breeze
Leaves on trees and bushes will constantly flutter. There are large wavelets in the water. Crests begin to break, with the possibility of scattered white horses. 'White horses' is a description of the white foam on waves, and I loved this description.

3. Beaufort 8 – Fresh Gale
Also referred to as just Gale, but I liked the idea that a force so strong it makes the top of skyscrapers sway was described as fresh.

Back in London, I started using the Beaufort scale to rate Rose's moods. Whenever I spoke to Judith on the phone and she asked me how Rose was, I would reply in Beaufort, saying things like 'She's well, just Beaufort 3 today' or 'Beaufort 7, I'd stay clear'. If I said 'Beaufort 12', she would ask to speak to Rose herself, so I tried to keep the numbers in the lower to mid range.

To this day, I can still recite the whole scale in the correct order. I suspect it's so ingrained in my memory that it will be the last thing to go, even if I forget everything else including my own name. The Beaufort scale has so far outlasted what should have been more enduring information, including the words to *Mary Had a Little Lamb*, the time of the last train home from London Bridge, and the name of the first boy I kissed (although I do remember he was an exchange student from Italy). The Beaufort scale even outlasted the hammock I sat in while memorising it, which was carried away by the wind a few summers later.

'At least it is not as windy as last week,' Uncle Jack said.

'I'm not sure the seagull outside would agree.'

'What seagull?' Jack lit up at the unforeseen twist in the wind conversation. I explained to him about the seagull, which had been thrown off course and was travelling in mostly unintended directions.

'You know, the wind is sometimes so strong that it knocks over large ships. So what chance does a small seagull have?'

'Uncle Jack, I have seen the seagulls on this island. They are the size of ships! What are you feeding them?'

'Obnoxious teenagers from London,' Judith chimed in.

'Is that why you're fattening me up?'

'Ah, now she knows my evil plan. I'd better go and check on lunch so we can start the force-feeding,' she said and got up from the sofa, collecting all the empty cups on her way out.

'Well, I hate this windy weather. I don't know how you put up with it.'

'It can be tiring. But without the strong winds, we would not have ended up here. Right, Judith?'

'Yes, Jack, you're absolutely right,' my grandmother replied as the door closed behind her.

The story of how Judith had arrived on the island and met my grandfather was one of Jack's favourites. Before he married Jane and still lived with Judith, we would stay up late some evenings and make Judith tell *The Most Romantic Story of all Time* (which, after he met Jane, was reclassified as *The Second Most Romantic Story of all Time*). It was one of many stories that Judith told us, and now I knew there were many more she hadn't. I almost asked Uncle Jack if he knew Judith had a sister, but I felt it would be a betrayal of her secret if he didn't.

'I should go,' Uncle Jack said and got up from the sofa.

I walked him to the door and said goodbye. Later that evening, he came back with Jane and they ate dinner with us. That night, he made Judith tell us the *The Second Most Romantic Story of all Time* again, which she did. She even told some other ones. The story she didn't tell was the one about a young woman named Judith and her sister, Hanna, who both loved the same boy.

The Inheritance Powder

Hilary Standing

Prologue

Arsenic is versatile. It has many forms. It kills quickly. It kills slowly. It makes the face look beautiful. It disfigures the skin. It is the only effective remedy for sleeping sickness. It is a homeopathic remedy for diarrhoea. Taxidermists used arsenic to preserve animal skins and to keep pests at bay. Its colouring properties caused the European wallpaper industry to boom – and the vapours killed uncounted numbers of their customers and their customers' children. Until the advent of forensic testing it was a fast and foolproof way to secure an early inheritance.

*

In a poor country like Bangladesh there are many bad deaths. In ancient, overcrowded ferries that sink, in shock from septicaemia after childbirth without any health care, under collapsed buildings made of shoddy cement and with no foundations, in fires that sweep through flimsy shacks; death from waves and cyclones and cold and heat. It seemed particularly unfair, he reflected afterwards, that an accident of geology added slow poisoning by arsenic.

Chapter One

Carl Simonovsky was thinking about the chemistry of soil fertilisers as he inspected his trilliums on a late May morning. He was conducting his routine round of the shaded garden while he waited for his computer to warm up.

After an initial anxious, sickly period, the plants were pushing up strongly, bending slightly to the filtering light. The foliage was turning the ochre-green that heralds both bloom and senescence. He thought that the flowers were only days away from their debut. He straightened up, pushed flopping strands of hair out of his eyes and smiled to himself.

Returning to his computer, marooned on the kitchen table amid the detritus of breakfast and last night's supper, he checked his emails; the usual stuff – three advertisements for potency enhancing supplements, two invitations to reveal his bank account details to people who had suddenly acquired a few million dollars and an altruistic desire to share them with him, an update on his airmiles and a request from a student for some references on the economic prospects of Namibia. There was also one from Marianne. *Let her wait.* Then he noticed the email from Professor Sayers:

From: Director's Office
To: Carl Simonovsky
Date: 27 May 2003
Subject: An opportunity for you?

My dear Carl, this is apropos our discussion last week on your current difficulties re finding sufficient income generating work this year. I was talking to a chap I know in EUROPOV. They are looking for someone to do a quickie in Bangladesh. Something about the economic analysis of interventions for dealing with the arsenic situation – apparently there's lots of it in the groundwater there. I presume it's something to do with being a delta. Poor buggers – can't win can they? But anyway, I immediately thought of you. I know it's not your part of the world, and not exactly agriculture, but bound to be the same cost benefit stuff, do it with your eyes closed. What say? Only catch is they need it yesterday. I had the info faxed over. Can you come in today to pick it up? Regards, Hugh.

The message implied a choice he knew he did not have. It also meant foregoing the luxury of a day spent dressing-gowned and unshaven, moving at will between the computer and the garden. Tripping over the worn kitchen carpet that he never seemed to get round to replacing, he headed for the bathroom. He showered and shaved quickly, nicking his chin in several places. Back in the bedroom, the wardrobe yielded no ironed shirts. He had forgotten to call the agency about replacing his regular cleaner. He pulled on an almost respectable tee-shirt and left the house.

*

At some point between stepping out of the station and reaching the office Carl's spirits always sagged. If he thought about it, then it was where he stopped to buy his third copy of that week's Big Issue from Jimmy, the last of the regular vendors on his route. The road was a traffic-harried stretch of bleakness. And from Jimmy's patch the grey facade of the office of the Institute for Poverty Alleviation was first visible. *Oh the bunker.* The term had dropped straight into his head on his first day at work there – god, nearly 20 years ago. Built in the brutalist style of 1970s London architecture, the location had been chosen for its convenience to Heathrow airport. The business of 'Ippa', as the Institute was generally known, was in the poorer parts of the world, researching poverty trends and advising governments on how to improve the lot of their citizens. Its renowned economists, hurrying around the world, could leave the office with a bare half hour to their check-in time.

But the once smart suburb had declined into blight. Ippa reminded him of a stranded whale washed up on a large traffic island, surrounded by half-inhabited streets. The journey took him past boarded-up houses and abandoned cars. Its decay oppressed him. It felt unyielding to any strategy his mind could devise. The bunker itself was daubed regularly with graffiti, causing the bursar to rail at the local police-community liaison officer to 'do something about these illiterate louts'. Now, it seemed to him, the term bunker described more than just the architecture.

Fresh graffiti had appeared since he last went into the office. The word 'WANKERS' was scrawled in foot high letters by the entrance door. At least, he thought, they could spell it. Seeing the bursar in the reception area making an irritated phone call, he turned abruptly, took a longer route to collect the fax from Professor Sayers' secretary and went on to his room.

Its disarray never failed to surprise him. He made heroic efforts to keep on top of the filing but papers lay everywhere, as if scattered by a studious but careless poltergeist. Ignoring the mess as best he could he switched on the computer and then turned reluctantly to the fax.

From: Office of the European Agency for Poverty Reduction (EUROPOV)
Att: Professor Hugh Sayers, Ippa
Sender: Director, Asia Operations

Hugh – good to speak to you, here's the arsenic job, Grateful if you can follow up with your contact. Regards, Lars

> Consultant needed for assignment in Bangladesh.
> Task: undertake cost-benefit analysis of proposed EUROPOV supported interventions in arsenic mitigation. Advise on best policy options.
> Person required: Economist with minimum 10 years experience in cost-benefit analysis of environmental (water and sanitation) interventions. Experience of region preferred but not essential.
> Length: three weeks in-country plus 3 days report writing.
> Start date: as soon as possible.
> Send CV to Paoul Andersson marked arsenic – urgent.

He sighed. He was an agricultural economist who had spent his working life in the dry farming zones of Africa. He had never been to 'the region'. He had never heard of the arsenic crisis in Bangladesh, let alone had any idea about mitigating it. And he had grave doubts about cost-benefit analysis. What, he wondered, would he be expected to value a life at in a poor, crowded, disaster-prone country? However, he reminded himself that in the last year considerations of ignorance, ethics and scepticism had not stopped him from providing policy advice on economic regeneration of the tourist industry in Bosnia-Hercegovina and alternative strategies for financing hospital care in Kazakhstan. Indeed, to his chagrin as well as surprise, his reports had been very well received. He was building up a profile as a flexible consultant who could deliver what was needed.

He called the administration office. 'Hi Tahera, it's me flushed out of my garden at last. Can you pull out one of my CVs for me? Not the research one. I need the consultancy one that's got the highlighted section on policy advice to governments and international agencies. It's a bit urgent, I'll come by in a minute and give you the fax sheet and number.'

He could hear the smile in her voice. 'I thought you'd decided to give up on international development and open a nursery.'

'Now you're giving me dangerous ideas, I'd need to enlarge the garden a bit.' They both laughed.

For a few minutes, Carl watched the pair of strutting, cooing pigeons that had taken up residence on his window ledge. The bursar had sent out several reminders recently that 'pigeon nuisance must be reported immediately'. Ignoring these was one of his small acts of rebellion. Then he walked down two flights of stairs to the administration office.

It was a windowless cubby hole in the basement sandwiched

between the kitchen and the washrooms. Carl put his head round the door. There was barely room for the one cluttered desk. Tahera shone out of the gloom in a pale yellow jacket and blue chiffon scarf, her welcoming smile turned in his direction. *How does she manage to look so good and stay so cheerful?*

'Here's the CV. I've tidied it up a bit. Your dates were all out of date, if you know what I mean.'

'Yes I do, and thanks, and by the way it's for an assignment in your birthplace.'

Her eyes widened. You're going to Bangladesh?

'Well, possibly, they have to accept my CV first.'

'Oh that's really exciting. I can't believe it. Take me along as your assistant.'

'Wish I could, a local would be really helpful.'

She laughed. 'But I don't know it any better than you do, unless you count growing up in Tower Hamlets.'

'Well that's still a big step closer than where I start from.'

'Don't worry. If you go I'll ask my mum for some tips, although she'll probably expect you to bring back a jar of pickles in return.'

Carl handed the fax to her.

'Thanks, and here's your updated one.' She snapped the CV into his hand as if to seal the outcome on the spot.

Ndambi

Diriye Osman

Haram

My sister tells me I'm living in sin. 'Tis true. But she doesn't conk that this is *my* sin. She tells me it is haram for a woman to love another woman. 'Tis also true. But I don't need to hear it from her.

She calls me on a regular to scope the situation, to sniff traces of melancholy and dissatisfaction in my voice. But I'm a psychoanalyst and this is pop psychology 101. I see it played out like a Carry On film on my ward every day. It's a game for rookies.

'How're you?' she asks.

'I'm fine, hon,' I say in a warm voice. 'Na wewe?'

'Alhamdulilah,' she says, although her timbre is slightly shaky, desperate to conceal. 'What you been up to?'

'Working,' I say. 'Things are hectic but exciting.'

'Hmm.' This is not what she wants to hear. 'And what about – ?' She pauses, expecting me to finish her sentence. I let the silence drag until I can hear her shallow breathing through the receiver.

'Adrienne?' I finally say with a smile. 'She's great. So sweet and gentle and' – I sigh for a blissed-out effect – '*giving*. She makes me feel like I'm the centre of the earth, like nothing else matters. Alhamdulilah!'

The silence becomes sound. With just a few, carefully chosen words, I've made incisions into her vital organs. Brick by brick, her interior structure starts to crumble. That's when the sermon begins.

'Walaahi, I pray that you see the light,' she says with the faux-sympathy of the faux-pious. 'I pray that the shatan leaves your spirit; I pray that you find a man because lesbianialism can be cured. I *pray* that Allah cures you. I *pray*. All you need to do is to find a good man and settle down.'

'Like you, right?'

My sister never finished high school because she wanted to play house with an illiterate bundu-boy from Bosaaso, who subsequently made her drop five babies before she was thirty, before dumping her ass for an Egyptian teenager with an air-tight clit and cash to stash. But I don't state this. It's not my style.

'Abdi was a good father!' she fumes. 'He loved his kids!'

'Yes,' I say in a mellow voice. '*Loved.*'

My sister weighs my spite before she spits, 'Are you even human?'

'No,' I say. 'It's probably my *lesbianialism*. I think its fucking up the rotation.'

'Maybe you need to check into a mental hospital.'

'Darling!' I gasp. 'Why you hurt me so? You know those places freak me out!'

'Hmmff! You shall chew lock one of these days.'

'Sister girl, I *always* chew lock, especially when you bell me. But you know how we do. We *maintain*.'

'No, sis,' she says, '*you* maintain while the rest of us carry bare burden.'

'Hawa,' I say, 'what do you want me to do for you?'

'I want – ' she sighs, 'I want you to say it'll be fine.'

'It'll be fine,' I say sincerely.

'How do you know?'

'I just do.'

She sighs a little more easily.

'How are the kids?' I ask.

'Alhamdulilah.'

'Tell them habo Ndambi will be over soon.'

'Ati Ndambi?' she sneers. 'Samira, when are you going to get real? Nobody calls themselves "Ndambi". Why'd you want to go from Samira to "Sin"?'

'It's "Ndambi", not "dhambi". It means "most beautiful".'

'Oh please!' she says.

'Bye Hawa.' I smile and hang up. After I put down the receiver I recline in my chair. I can hear one of my patients playing 'Young Hearts Run Free' in their room. I prick up my ears, let the rhythm ride my pulse. Candi Staton got it right when she sang about self-preservation.

Night-time

When I come home that evening, I listen to my answering machine. There are no messages from Adrienne. I chuckle sadly to myself.

Night-time is always the hardest. It's when the ghouls of my imagination play games with my sanity. So I get practical and run a bath. I fill the steaming water with oils and salts until the tub is slick. Adrienne used to do this for me every night after I came home from work. She used to buy 'bath bombs' which were fruity soaps that dissolved effervescently in water. I would emerge from the bathroom smelling of mango and sexual hunger.

We would kiss like love-starved youts. She would press me hard against the wall, lick my lips, tongue would meet tits, hips, clit. She would melt me down until I stunk of sex and satisfaction. And then we would lie in bed and talk of all the love we had gained and everything we had lost. Those conversations were our way of fortifying the chord that connected us. What was once our temple, the place where we created love, has become my fortress, a space custom-built for turmoil. So what to do? Should I sink further into funk and act stone-face outside these walls? Should I continue to not mention my loss to anyone?

Or…

Should I come harder?

I decide these questions don't need answers tonight. Tonight is about TV and takeaway and bourbon on ice. It's about dabbing attar on my collarbone and cotton sheets. Tonight is a date with Maxwell and Coco de Mer.

I remove my bra and panties, enjoy the curve of my breasts, the groove of my nipples. I squeeze the tips, feel them tighten. I run my palm under my powder-soft arms, massage each muscle until I moan. My body has not been touched in moons and tonight I want to sweat, shimmer. My mind plays games with my body, directing my fingertips to the nook of my navel. But I don't fully touch skin. Instead, I suck my stomach in and close my eyes. I focus on my breathing.

I inhale.

Hold.

Release.

I do this until I am loose.

It is time.

Love Egg

I walk over to my closet and remove the box. It is black and the gold-leaf card attached to it reads:

The Jade Love Egg practice originated in ancient China. Taoist Masters taught the secrets of the Jade Egg only to a very small number of women: the Empress and the concubines. It was believed that these practices gave them longevity, youthful energy and extraordinary skills as lovers.

I carry the box to my bed. I lay it down and reach for the Arabian oils on my bedside table. I rub the oils all over myself. The scent is musk and morning glory. I sprawl on the bed and open my thighs wide while Maxwell's 'Embrya' steams up the room. Maxwell's falsetto is cream on wax and as I coax one, two, three fingers inside my pussy, my toes curl. As I go deeper within myself the music sounds richer and the musk smells sweeter. I push my hips back and forth to take in my fingers. When I'm wet I wipe my hands on a towel. I open the Coco de Mer box and remove the jade egg. It is smooth, shaped like a duck egg. I put it in my mouth to moisten it. As Maxwell's bass-line becomes my heartbeat, I drop the egg onto my palm. I trace it around my nipples, torso and pubic bone, which glisten with oil and sweat. I tease myself like this until my throat is dry, until I'm panting.

I'm tight so I slowly twerk the egg inside me. It's painful at first but I open up as I gently push and pull the semi-precious stone. The room feels so hot I can barely breathe. I inhale and exhale at a deep, hypnotic pace. I imagine Adrienne's tongue on my clit and my body starts building up to climax, until I can no longer control my breath, until all I can do is howl. When I come, the love egg pops out of me and I simply lie there, legs shaking. After I shower and drift off to sleep, Maxwell's 'Embrya' comes to an end. The final track is a recording of an ultrasound. The last thing I hear that night is a baby's heart beating inside my head.

Freedom

The prophet once said that dreams are a window into the unseen. I have been told many times by family, friends, colleagues and strangers, that I, a black African, Muslim lesbian, am not included in this vision; that my dreams are a reflection of my upbringing in a decadent, amoral Western society that has corrupted who I really am. But who am I, really? Am I allowed to speak for myself or should my desires form the battleground for causes I do not care for? My answer to that is simple: 'no one *allows* anyone anything.' By rejecting that notion, you discover that only you can give yourself permission on how to lead your life, naysayers be damned. In the end, something gives way. The earth doesn't move but something shifts. That shift is 'change' and 'change' is the layman's lingo for that elusive state that lovers, dreamers, prophets and politicians call 'freedom'.

Do I think I'm free? Well, let a sister break it down for ya. I often dream of home. It is a place that exists only in my imagination: it is my Eden, my Janna. Sometimes I associate it with my father, my mother, my grandmother, my sister, all of whom have rejected me, all of whom I still love. Sometimes home takes the shape of my ex, Adrienne. I like to think that the memory of her beautiful Afro, spiky attitude and sweetness is sacred, that I worship at her altar. Other times, I regard Somalia, my birthplace, as home, as the land where my soul will eventually be laid to rest. Many times home is Kenya or London. But none of these places or people truly *embody* home for me. Home is in my hair, my lips, my arms, my thighs, my feet and hands. I am my own home. And when I wake up crying every morning, thinking of how lonely I am, I pinch my skin, tug at my hair, remind myself that I am alive. Remind myself to step outside and greet the morning. Remind myself that it's all about forward motion. It's all about change. It's all about that elusive state.

Freedom.

Selected Poems

Kayo Chingonyi

Daemon

I often think I see you reflected
in the buffed sheen of a night
library's desk, but it is usually
some drunken fool with enough
presence of mind to slide an entry
pass along its scanner, shamble
these aisles to disturb us: the hard-
core essayists, those who wait till
the dawn sun sneaks its hot breath
up the back of a tense neck to call
the thing attempted finished.
                       No surprise
I can't catch you unawares at the
edge of this dark river. You know
I wish you dead that I might plumb
the nether depth I should have left
with Lego blocks and questions.
The closest I can ever get is to have
you sit with me. Though you are no
totem I observe you with the same
amazement of that first day when
a stick, held above the blank sand
twitched, its slight tremor
                       just palpable.

RSVP

I know I'm somewhat under-dressed but I was forced to throw something together at the last minute since I had to find out second hand from Phyllis that it was all happening today and owing to some difficulties I won't go into now my invitation didn't reach me in time but, such occasions being something of a rarity these days, what with the casual ways of our young people and the filth that gets played on the radio, what I mean to say is you expect something for your trouble turning down a round of golf at Crowland's Heath and coming halfway across the country as I've done. To think I taught the groom to tie a double Windsor knot. Well, if I'm not welcome. No, don't put yourself out on my account, I wouldn't dream of trespassing on your precious time a moment longer.

Promise

You told me it was the last
time; that I'd never taste
Marlboros
      on your breath or inhale
the scent of another's caress
at your nape, again.

So when I ask you to explain
this alien musk lining your coat
and you say *it's nothing*
      I believe you; leave doubt
to watch us and wait
for a suitable time to interject.

Kenta
After Breton

Kid brother, with the chicken bone knuckles/uranium skin/eyes of white glass/face
of cold steel/feet of small bear/teeth of smashed crockery/kiss of Ndola mist/voice
of wisps/head of clumps and patches/belly of warm dough/odour of burning/fingers
of crackled peat/chest of cypress wood/thoughts of mango of guava of cassava/smile
of snapped elastic/face of chalk/face of cracked wafer/name of blown eardrum/steps
of falling ash/breath of jet/mwaice wandi, second born, with a heart of bad arithmetic.

Baltic Mill
for Hannah

Though you maintain the elements
have conspired against us we still
inch the cobbled street past Castle
Keep down to the Quayside's rain
slick paving slabs all for the whim
of standing across from Baltic Mill
in a turbid mist lifted from the Tyne.

We planned to catch a talk at the Laing
or the Biscuit but, pushed for time,
plumped for a backstreet pizzeria, throw-
back to another world, a haberdasher's
maybe or greasy spoon for blackface
minstrels from Gateshead mines and
iron works. The North Sea wind-chill

bids us leave behind this city of faces
cast in stories passed down, vestige
of years when hundreds of miles stood
between us. The exact course that brought
us here is unimportant. It is that we met
like this river, drawn from two sources,
offered up our flaws, our sedimental selves.

calling a spade a spade

My agent says I have to use my street voice.
Though my talent is for rakes and fops I'll drop
the necessary octaves, stifle a laugh
at the playwright's misplaced *get me bluds* and *safes*.
If I get it they'll ask how long it takes me
to grow *cornrows* without the small screen's knowing
wink. Three years rada, two years rep and I'm sick
of playing *lean dark men who might have guns*.
I have a book of poems in my rucksack,
blank pad, two pens, tattered A-Z, headphones
that know Prokofiev as well as Prince Paul.

Eau de Vie

Eamonn Doran

I lived in a district of Paris that had tight narrow streets, where the cafes, bars, restaurants and boutiques bulged to the corners of each block. It was nothing like the great boulevards of the Haussmann Paris. In the summer it was packed with tourists, but in the winter it was grey and quiet, almost peaceful.

My apartment was in a two-storey annexe built into a courtyard off Rue C------. On the ground floor was a repair shop. The two grimed widows, either side of the door, were filled with broken woodwind instruments. Both were devoted to piccolos, which were piled on the inside sill like blackened bones studded with brass. I lived on the first floor and had to enter the courtyard to get to my door.

For the first month, the apartment above mine was unoccupied. That changed when I walked into the courtyard and opened the door to the annexe, climbed the narrow cold stairs that no-one else ever seemed to use to the first floor, turned the key in my front door, and heard someone shuffle on the stairs above. I delayed pushing the door open and, leaving the key in the lock, listened with one ear cocked. Slowly, a man turned the corner of the stair. As he came from the shadow, he was watching his feet and placed every step with care. With the appearance of an insect walking upright, he held the rail with three gnarled fingers. A plastic bag was gripped around his thumb. It was impossible to guess his age. I pushed my door open.

'Bonjour,' he said as he took the last few steps.

'Bonjour, monsieur,' I said.

When he got to my level I could see his eyes like blue glass shining beneath a head of cropped, light red hair.

'Je m'appelle Daniel.' I heard the word Daniel crash its alien sound at the end of the sentence whenever I said it after speaking French.

'Daniel, ah, you moved in while I was away. And where do you come from Daniel, or is it Danny?' he said, switching to English.

'That's complicated,' I said.

'Complicated? I like you already Danny. You don't mind Danny, do you?' he asked. I had not been called Danny since I was a child, and that was only by my mother.

'No, of course not,' I said.

'Good, my name is Marco.' He placed the plastic bag at his feet.

'Good to meet you, Monsieur Marco,' I said. I felt awkward. He burst into a laugh.

'Monsieur Marco, I like that. It reminds me of a young woman, a long time ago, and a song she used to sing. That was a long time ago, but I like that...Monsieur Marco!' he looked at the ground as his laugh faded. I wondered if I should invite him in or just leave this as a casual passing on the stair. But he picked up his bag and moved past me.

'You must come up for a glass of wine. It is good for neighbours to know a little of each other.' He stopped and smiled. 'Come up tomorrow at six, if you are free?'

'Yes, I will...eh,' I was unsure how to address him.

'You can call me Marco, but I like Monsieur Marco. It makes me smile, you know, inside,' he said. His eyes looked into mine. I felt I was being hypnotised.

'Monsieur Marco,' I said, 'see you tomorrow.'

'A demain, et merci.... Monsieur Marco, that makes me smile, thank you,' he said as he passed by me. He descended the final stair smiling and speaking softly to himself.

*

Ever since I had moved in, there had been a heady curious odour in the little annex. As I walked up the blue painted concrete steps to M. Marco's little studio the odour grew. I stood in front of the door for a moment. I knocked. M. Marco opened the door, which made a cautious creak. One blue eye appeared around the initial opening. He looked behind me and down the dark stairs before pulling the door fully. He beckoned me into the room. It was lit as if by amber.

I found the source of the odour. It was an oil lamp on the semi-circle of drop-leaf table to the right that was tight against the wall. The lamp, a thick column of brass with a simple yellow glass cover for the flame, was the only source of light. Beside the lamp was a plain green wine bottle with no label. M. Marco pointed at one of the two old thin armchairs that were by the table. I sat in the one he had assigned to me, while he sat in the one that faced the door. He reached down, and from a box under the table produced two small wine glasses.

'You drink, yes?' he said while pouring.

'Yes.'

I looked around the room, though I tried not to look like I was doing so. There was a folded cot-bed against the far wall beside a window. Thin muslin curtains draped the window with a line of dust on the folds, caught between the light of the lamp and the faded daylight from the courtyard. The only electronic device was an old radio. When I turned to Marco he was looking at me as if he was reading my thoughts:

'I don't like to have too much things. They weigh me down, even when I am not here. The idea of things waiting for me...weighs on me, yes.' He handed me a glass.

'Now tell me, Danny, your story. How long have you been here?'

'A few weeks,' I said, as the wine coated my mouth with luxury.

'Ah, very good. Have you met any of our other neighbours in the building opposite?' He sipped and looked at the table.

'No, you're the first I've spoken to.'

'I am honoured. So tell me of you. What has you in Paris? I recall you said your life was complicated?'

'Oh,' I said and paused with the usual frantic scramble in my mind to find the easiest way to explain my history, 'I grew up in Portugal and in the south, here, in France, and my parents...' I gave up.

Marco, seeing my discomfort, interjected. 'You are a nomad?' he said smiling. He refilled our glasses.

'Yes, that is exactly what I am,' I said with relief. That was it. In one simple word he had summed up, not only my existence, but what beat in my heart every day. But the irony was that I was in Paris to find a place to root, to stop. But I didn't want to tell him that then. In the amber light and his eyes of blue glass, he had made me fall in love with being a nomad, even if that nomad longed to be still.

'I am glad to hear it. You can trust a nomad. Though, these days the world seems to be of the contrary opinion. But I do not trust a man committed to stay in one place. No, no I do not. He has too much to lose to be trusted. But a nomad has no reason to lie to you, or to tell you the truth for that matter. You take him as he comes. It is as simple as that. And I shall take you as you come...and I hope you will do me the same courtesy. A toast then, but I have a better bottle for this.' He pushed himself upright with his thin arms. He returned with a bottle of clear spirit. *Eau de vie*.

He sat and from the box beneath the table pulled out two small, neat glasses wedged either side of his swollen knuckled middle finger. He laid them on the table. Once he had poured the drinks, he raised his glass.

'To all the nomads,' he said with his chin raised like an old soldier at a memorial service.

I drank. The liquid burned a line down my throat and dropped a small ball of fire into my belly. I exhaled, my mouth open, and felt warm in that light and the blue eyes of M. Marco.

'Do you have any family, Danny?' He refilled the glasses. I wanted to decline, but I didn't want to appear impolite.

'Yes, my mother. She lives in the south. My father died when I was a teenager.' I left it at that, and he didn't pry any further. 'What about you?' I felt bold in asking him anything, as he seemed the sort of man that liked to ask questions rather than answer them. But the *eau de vie* had done its job.

'Oh,' he said shifting in his chair and looking down onto the table, 'my life is a simple one. I have no family – sometimes it is a curse, sometimes a blessing, I never know which most of the time. But I have many friends. I am lucky that way. Yes, I have some very good friends. So, all in all, I would say I am a lucky man. I have been a lucky man. I meet people like you Danny!' He smiled and poured another. 'In fact, I have to meet some of these people later, so I'm afraid I will have to go soon. But we can do this again, no?'

I agreed, and about half an hour later we left his studio together. He let me go ahead, but when we got to the turn on the stairs he said he had forgotten something. I waited at my door. He arrived a moment later with a leather bag over his left shoulder.

'Good night, Danny. I will see you soon again, I hope.'

'Bonsoir, Monsieur Marco,' I said with a smile.

We shook hands and Marco descended the final flight of stairs.

From the courtyard, I heard him laugh in the warm air of the late September evening. Through the open window that carried Marco's laugh, the lavender planted below filled my apartment with scent

That night, as I lay in bed and looked around my small single bedroom, I reflected on the studio above: the smell of the lamp, its amber light, the table, the cot and the calm. My reflections were shattered by a truck that passed by on the narrow street. It created a minor tremor that shook the room. I felt it in my body through the iron frame of the bed. The truck passed, and the room stilled. But the tremor still stirred in my chest. I was drawn to the reflection of my bedside lamp on the honey coloured veneer of the wardrobe. My thoughts returned to Marco. Perhaps, it was my own bent for a Spartan life that led me to an instant affection for him. Maybe, it was his hypnotic eyes and ease of manner that enticed you to reveal yourself. And though I came north to Paris to find my own life, my own freedom, not desiring anyone else's company, Marco's presence opened me up.

The tremor in my chest subsided. I felt like I was dissolving into the grey light of room. I turned to lie on one side, then the other. Finally, I lay on my back. I felt my naked body beneath the sheet. I could feel my fingertips on my groin and the tops of my thighs. My skin tingled at their touch. I could feel the tug on some tiny hairs when my fingertips moved. I could feel my heart beat against my breast bone. I kept my eyes open and breathed.

Too, too much of the world, the past, filtered through a crack with amber light and was let into my slight mind...

Man, Walking

Sally Skinner

Burgundy, 1904, some weeks after the death of Étienne-Jules Marey, the physiologist who spent his life recording movement in all its forms. His daughter, Francesca, is lost in grief. This extract comes from near the beginning of the novel, which is provisionally titled The Fleeting.

The house in Chagny is large and quiet. A place of echoes, despite the impression of solidity. It sits squarely on its hill like a sculptor's block of sandstone, white-shuttered windows overlooking the fields of vines my father helped to plant. In a fit of lyricism he named our winery after a local legend that tells of witches and fairies meeting there. *Domaine de la Folie*: a name belonging to a mythical time of songs and spells and rustlings that's hard to imagine in this quietude. A narrow lane leads up to the house, winding through the copse where we built the observation towers. Often, when the air is still, the only sound to be heard from the house is the birdsong that pours from the pine trees.

The funeral rites are over. The servants have been dismissed. Noel and I move about the rooms in our separate worlds, occasionally alerted to each others' presence by the whispers of the house. Water filling the bathtub; shoes on the stairs; the dull thud of a knife chopping potatoes on the other side of a wall.

I'm on the upstairs landing when I hear the front door swing open and shut. I feel it, too, in my bare feet. A moment later Noel appears on the drive, then moves out of sight. We've hardly spoken for days now and I don't know if it's tact that has caused him to withdraw from me, or exasperation. I've lost my father, not a spouse. Not a child. Papa's death was expected, even wished for at the end. Is this what my husband is thinking?

I move closer to the window so I can see him again. He walks straight across my field of vision, exactly as if he were the subject of a chronophotograph, and I feel my father's presence beside me. Noel's straw hat obscures his face, but I can read his state of mind in the motions of his body, as clear as any sentence. He's tired.

It was through Papa we first met. He'd searched Noel out after admiring some of his frescos in the Gare de Lyon and found they had a common interest in heraldic painting. When Noel first called on us at the Boulevard Delessert, I'd thought him just another troubled young artist. In spite of my efforts to put him at ease whilst Papa finished his work, he seemed to have difficulty meeting my eye, preferring to fix his gaze on the rim of his hat which he turned round and round in his hands. Over later encounters I came to realise he was shy with young women, having spent little time in their company, and it became my project to befriend him. I fell in love with the slow unfurling of his nature as much as that nature itself. He was gentle. He was witty. He talked to me about the painting of horses, the precise quality of Italian sunlight, the artistic importance of my father's work. He laughed affably at my watercolours. I never felt a burning attraction to his slight frame, but I liked his pointed beard and dancing grey eyes.

I watch my husband walking across the drive and recognise his exhaustion as my own. Beyond that, it's impossible to say what he's thinking. He was so happy when I told him we were expecting a child. Now he continues to walk away from the house, following the lane down towards the copse. I open the window and lean out to keep sight of him: a shrinking figure in white against the dark green of the pines. If he looked back now he would see a figure in black emerging from the pale gold of the house.

'Noel.'

His name cracks in my mouth. I try again but find I cannot shout and my husband disappears into the trees.

Mamma believed that thirteen was too old to be climbing trees, but Mamma was back in Posillipo.

I was by the track outside the *Station Physiologique*, appraising the trunk of an ash for potential footholds, when something in the middle distance caught my eye, something upright and blazing white against the blackness of the hangar. At first I thought it might be a statue, though I couldn't imagine why it would have been placed there. But much had happened in the week since my arrival and I'd learnt not to be surprised by anything at the *Station*. I barely flinched when the statue began to move.

It was a man, I realised, but a man so tightly clad in white his form was shockingly revealed. I hid myself behind the tree trunk and considered this mirage of nudity. He was taller than my father and even Georges. Wide, muscular shoulders tapered to a solid waist, and the cleft of his back directed my scrutiny to the switching spheres of his buttocks, which propelled him forward in time with a thunderous beat.

I glanced towards the centre of the field. The beat was coming from a mechanical drum, apparently designed to measure out his paces. Between the drum and the hangar, my father was taking his position in the mobile wagon that contained his photographic equipment. Emboldened by the sight of him, I ran across the field to enter the wagon.

'Who is your subject today, Papa?' I asked, resting my hand on his shoulder as he prepared the apparatus. He turned to me with an expression of impatience, but it quickly softened.

'Ah, Cesca. This is Monsieur Schenkel. I shall introduce you to him once we're finished here. One of the finest cadets from Joinville, I'm told.' He looked at me with amusement. 'Quite a specimen, don't you think?'

I felt myself begin to blush and looked away. 'Tell me about the experiment, Papa.'

'Well, it rather depends who you're talking to. The Ministry of War believe we're providing the objective, scientific foundation they need to reform the army. Still smarting from Prussia, you see. They're determined they won't be defeated again.' His voice dwindled to a mutter as he dropped a slotted disk into his camera.

'And aren't you?'

'What's that?'

'Helping to reform the army.'

'Oh yes, they'll get what they need. Chronophotographs documenting every kind of pace and exercise you can imagine. Which pace will carry our young friend the greatest distance in the shortest time. Which with the least fatigue. Which drills will best develop his stamina, and so on.' He gave a small snort of laughter. 'And I'll get what I need, too.'

I didn't have to ask what that was, for it was always the same: to capture fleeting movement, the manifestation of life itself, as a lasting trace.

'I let Georges see to the official side of things,' he said with lowered voice, though there was no chance of anyone hearing our conversation. 'Application is all well and good, but it's the principle, the truth that we must work towards.'

I realised he was looking at me intently. 'Yes, Papa.'

Presently, he sat his apparatus in motion and instructed Schenkel to walk in front of the hangar. I watched the white figure march, jog and run across the camera's field of vision, left to right, left to right, over and over again, like something moving endlessly across an urn. The virtuosic movement continued until the sun slipped behind a cloud and obliged the athlete to loiter a while in the shadows.

My father directed my attention to an album of chronophotographs. Duplicate images of another Joinville gymnast strode like ghosts across the black strip of the hangar. Each figure depicted a new phase in the march, the swinging arms and legs fanning out from points of stasis, the cadence of limbs captured in pedantic detail. The prints were impeccably catalogued. *Walk; Run; Jump; Walk up an Incline; Run up an Incline; Jump from an Incline onto a Pile of Hay.* And suddenly a now-familiar face: *Georges Demenÿ Playing the Violin.* I laughed at the incongruity, nearly causing my father to drop the celluloid plate. Excusing myself, I put the album away and jumped down from the wagon.

In my room that night, I threw open the window and stretched out on the bed. The pages of my journal lay spread open in front of me. I had only to close my eyes and I could hear Monsieur Schenkel's voice, reproduce in my mind the exact angle of his jaw, feel the hotness that flushed my cheeks when my father introduced us. But there was no language sufficient to describe these things, any more than there were words to capture the motions of my own heart.

I closed the book and contented myself with replaying in my mind's eye what I'd seen from the wagon, discovering that I could accelerate the soldier-athlete movements, or retard them to ridiculous slowness, or even freeze them long enough to drink in every delicious detail of the sight of *Man, Walking*. I saw again the right knee lifting, left arm swinging forward, the vertical of his body tilting slightly as if about to fall. The white attire blazing in the midday sunlight. The curves and inclines of shoulderblade, waist, buttock, thigh, calf. How funny that I could have such an unwitting plaything! And how pathetic.

Wolf Winter

Cecilia Ekback

In 1869, the Pentecostal preacher Daniel Bred comes to the remote Blackåsen Mountain in Swedish Lapland to convert the settlers. Not many weeks after his arrival, one of the settlers is found savagely killed and the settlers who have so far kept to themselves are forced together by the event. Soon the mountain is alive with rumours. Having seen up close what fear can do to communities, one of the local settler women, Maj Heikkinen, sets out to discover the truth, sensing that what is at stake is more than one man's death. For to Blackåsen most settlers have come fleeing someone or something, and fear is too good a breeding ground for evil.

Part I

Blackåsen Mountain, Swedish Lapland, June 1865

'But how far is it, Frederika. Exactly?'

Frederika wanted to scream out loud. Marit was slowing them down. She dragged behind her the branch she ought to be using as a whip and Frederika had to work twice as hard to keep the goats moving. The morning was bright. White daylight sliced the spruce tops and stirred up too much colour. Frederika was hot. There were prickles on her back beneath the dress. The only sounds were those of a spruce tree shifting, of a hoof striking stone and the constant blah-blah bleating of the stupid goats.

'Only poor people have goats,' she had declared to her mother that morning.

Her mother raised an eyebrow.

'At least cows and sheep manage on their own in the forest. Goats are a lot of work for nothing.'

'Patience, Frederika,' her mother cautioned, eyebrow still raised. 'It's only for a few days until the fence around the field is repaired. You can take them to the glade. It's not far.'

Frederika hadn't said anything more. She could tell from the dark line above her mother's brow it was no use.

'How far, Frederika? How far? How far? How far?'

'Walk,' Frederika said.

She had answered the question already a hundred times.

This morning was the worst ever. Like every summer, in early June they had dressed the cottage in finest summer wear – rinsed the walls, scrubbed the floor with birch twigs under their feet until its wood was white, lifted out the windows and washed them, stuffed fresh rags around them when they put them back in and scrubbed the furniture with soap – on top, inside, underneath. When all was clean, they chalked the timber walls and then moved out.

Summ-mumm-mumm-er.

The only time of year they didn't have to work, eat and sleep all together in the one room. At night, their mother played their summer game, 'So where will you sleep tonight?' And the children tried to come up with the strangest sleeping place.

Only last night Marit had said: 'I will sleep wherever Frederika sleeps.'

Behind her little sister, her mother tilted her head, pursed her lips, made the begging eyes. *Aw. Pu-hlease? Just this one night?*

And Frederika had given in. Big mistake. It turned out that Marit was rotten in bed. She moved around in her sleep and babbled, as if she were awake. When it was time to get up, Frederika was so tired she wanted to smack her sister.

Then they had barely begun to walk when Marit needed to pee. Her sister whimpered and whined. *This wasn't a good spot. Here were too many mosquitoes... Ajjj! She had stepped on a horrible twig.*

Frederika waited on the trail. A black and white striped beetle climbed a trunk, probably on its way to work. She leaned forward, poked at it before squashing it with her finger. Then she felt appalled, wished the deed undone.

'How far?' Marit said again.

Frederika looked at the blonde tot beside her, too little for the inherited dress that stood around her like a sheet on a clothesline in wind. Marit stumbled on the trailing hem. 'Lift your feet when you walk and hurry.'

'But I am tired, Frederika. Frederika, I'm tired, I'm tired, I'm tired.'

It was going to be an awful, awful day.

As they came near the glade, Frederika sensed rather than saw it at first. She stopped. The goats sensed it too, hesitated, stared at her and bleated large question marks. It was something to do with the smell, she thought. Frederika knew the smell. It was that of slaughter: earth, rot, faeces. Something had died close by.

She waved away a fly which buzzed by her ear. There was a bundle at the far end of the glade, a deer perhaps, or a reindeer. She put her finger in front of her mouth. 'Shhh,' she whispered to Marit.

Marit grabbed her hand and stepped close. Frederika looked around like her mother had taught her. In the forest there was plenty of both bear and wolf. Whatever had attacked could still be about. She concentrated and listened. The tap of a woodpecker. The sun burning on her scalp. Marit's hand, sticky, twitching in hers. Nothing else. She looked back towards the bundle.

But that couldn't be an animal, that bundle was blue.

She let go of Marit and took a step forward. Marit followed and grabbed at her hand again.

There was a man on the ground in the glade. He stared at Frederika with cloudy eyes. He lay strangely – bent, flat, motionless. His stomach was torn open and his insides were on the grass beside him. And at once it was upon her, Marit screaming, the stench, the flies, the man's gaping mouth.

O, Jesus, please help, she thought. *Please help.*

They had to get their father. *Jesus.* They couldn't just leave him. And the goats. The goats would never stay together in one place.

She squatted down, grabbed her sister's shoulders and turned her around with force. Marit's eyes were round, her mouth wide open, strings of saliva between top and bottom which became a bubble, then popped. She lost her breath and her mouth gawped in horrid silence.

'Marit,' she said. 'Marit, I must fetch Father. Stay here with the goats and I'll run.'

Marit clambered up her like a cat up a tree, clawing. Frederika tried to loosen her sister's arms. 'Shhhhh.'

She stood up. 'It's okay,' she said with a voice so steady it surprised her. 'We shall all go.'

It is shortest through the Goat's Pass, she thought.

The forest had fallen quiet. There was no rustling, no tapping, murmuring, or chirping. There was no movement, either. It was as if the forest held its breath. What if… What if the killer *was* still there? Frederika reached for Marit's hand.

Marit was still screaming. She now bent her knees as if to sit down. Frederika yanked her to her feet. 'Run,' she hissed. Her sister didn't move. 'Run!' Frederika yelled and raised her hand as if to hit her.

Marit gasped and set off down the trail. Frederika spread her arms wide and ran towards the goats. 'Run!' she shouted. 'Run!'

They flew through the forest. Hoofs and bare feet drummed against the trail. Every sound was that of a predator: hounding, trailing, hunting them as it had stalked the man in the glade. 'Faster!' Frederika yelled and whipped whosoever's bottom was last. At one point she fell, knees stinging, hands scraping. *Up-up-don't-stop*. Then one of the goats jumped off the trail. She screamed in frustration and slapped its rear with her two bare hands.

When they reached the Goat's Pass, Frederika grabbed Marit's arm, held her back. 'We must be quiet,' she whispered. Marit hiccupped and dry-sobbed. Her eyes flickered. Frederika pinched her and she opened her mouth to let out a howl. Frederika put her hand over her sister's mouth and pleaded, close to tears herself now, 'I'm sorry. Marit, please, please, just a little bit longer.'

She stretched out her hand. *Please*. Her sister took it. They followed the goats into the pass. One step, two, three.

Nothing felt longer than walking through the Goat's Pass. And yet there was not much to it: the trail on the mountain's side dipped a little, perhaps it narrowed too. To the left, there was the same old valley. But to the right, the side of the mountain had burst and a fracture cut deep into it. And from inside this crack Frederika had heard noises. Not bumbling animal twangs, no, these were evil sounds, of breathing, of something wrestling to break loose. Made her skin pull together tight.

Don't look, Frederika thought, and kept her eyes on her feet. Four, five, six. Through the corner of her eye she saw Marit's naked feet on the trail beside hers half-walking, half-running.

Seven, eight, nine. The goats' hoofs were loud against the rocks. *Clop-Clopp-CLOPPETY. Please*, she thought. *Pleasepleaseplease.* Ten.

The path twisted and slackened and then flattened and fell downwards and outwards and they began to run – slowly at first, then faster. Downhill now, sighting the house between the trees. Marit ahead of her, screaming, *Mamma! Mamma!*

And at last, safe in their yard, their parents running towards them, her father with long strides, her mother, lifting her skirt, one hand under the large stomach. Then Frederika vomited.

Her father reached her, hauled her up by her arm, 'What is going on?' His face was white. 'What happened?'

'Eriksson,' Frederika said and wiped her mouth, 'in the glade and he is dead.'

And then her mother swept her into her long skirts and Frederika decided to stay there and never emerge again.

Selected Poems

Helen Adie

Bodyscape

Our eyelashes fluttered,
birds and heart beats.
Fingers interlaced were
church and steeple,
a lofty nave, ribcage.
All the little people were
busy organs that pump
and sift and filter.
We craned our necks
to see our bodies
curve into landscape,
nose-diving down to our feet,
which now I look at
in the bath, pink toes
like rocks giving out
the last of the sun.

The Other

She asks of her body,
(which has turned
and postured as if
belonging to another)
to show her how it knows
to be. The hands reply:
one takes the other, fingers
folding round to close
the rest of her
inside.

Slate

Sharp triangle of slate, a heart
the length of your hand.

Scraped, it sounds of the land,
the stone; imagined sparks –

the first struck fire when
stone and slate made hearth.

Little boy blue

sat in a corner eating his mother away with the fairies. Soon he will gather to her like the dust, settling for questions. At meal times, the pitter patter of willow on the plate and the spool click spool click spool of time. There he is, making shadows for himself, his hand an animal. *Look, rabbit ears.* An arm curves to a swan neck *Look mum* spool click. She almost nods, her hand wiping surfaces. Dust sighs out. A gap opens up blue between them, and she grips the edge of the table to keep from spinning away with the...*Can we have that again?* a high voice says, again and again, the same story over as the knives click clatter in the drawer.

The Turn of the Nine Maidens

Year after year they tilt to the sky
rough weathering their circle
like witches slippered in heather.

The other night, the sky fell into flood pools
 around the Nine Maiden stones,
whose heads were used to butting it like seals.

Dizzy with contradiction – at clouds
marbling the water round their feet –
they dived into their own small moats.

We're mermaids! they shrieked,
(the heather shuddering),
See how our heads have turned to tails!

In Time

A stitch saves nine,
what? Lives
make a cat last
as long as batteries
or a piece of string.

    Grass grows slowly.
        Blades reach up for a lifting,
            landing dandelion.

Watch a clock and the hands
stay put, though time
sneaks out behind your back.

In time I will sing to you
Que sera sera,
rocking your red fist raging self
in the shattering hours.

Look how we move through it,
how the past scrolls before us,
the future skulks behind

and how many versions of you
there are in a tapering day.

Mantelpiece

Flotsam is almost orderly
in the room's filtered light;
picked off the beach,
shells and driftwood strew
the marble shelf as if
colluding.

       Your hand crabs
a silver flash between stone
greys – quick fish for an eye hook –
the beaten carcass of a can, bashed
surface glimmering as if the water
still washed over and over.

It won't last. We follow the sea,
discarding what we've found.

Étienne

Georgina Wolfe

Switzerland: 1973

Afterwards, sitting across the table from me in the gendarmerie, Monsieur le Commissaire told me to start at the beginning. Even now I am not sure where that was. Of course, we all knew where it ended. The body hanging matter-of-fact from the basket of the descending hot air balloon.

We followed the scream of his mother, for she had recognised his shoulders even as they sloped, a hundred feet up, beneath the broken neck. She had recognised the trace of hair, shading his chin and lip. She had recognised the slight flare of his trousers as the wind whipped them tight against his legs.

We followed as she chased after the balloon, at first through the streets and then, as the pavements ceased, across the grassy floodplain, through the fields, alongside the snaking river.

Though she must have been breathless from running – a short lady with a lifetime of cheese and wine stored on her thighs, hips, belly – she screamed as she ran; the animal wail of a mother I had not heard before or since.

The village men ran too, chasing the balloon with its trailing cargo like children pursuing an escaped kite. They tried shooting it down, aiming at the red silk with the rifles they used to shoot cattle. The first bullets whistled through the fabric, any hiss of hot air lost in the winds high above us. The balloon swept on.

Hearing the gunfire, the boy's mother stopped her pursuit and rounded on the men. Her screams were now an indecipherable mix of French and German. She spat at these armed men who took aim and fired too close to her swaying son. Monsieur Mönsch from the butchers reached her first and put out his arms to embrace her, ready to scoop her up like a wailing infant. But she did not stop. She had already whipped around. Monsieur Mönsch was left, empty-armed and foolish.

The chase continued. The balloon, wrinkling now, sank without its flow of hot air, only to be caught by a mischievous cross-wind and lifted high once more, high above our heads. The body suspended beneath jerked as the wind took hold. I wondered later if, with a last surge of life, the boy saw us running beneath him. Saw us running like ants, his line of pursuers trailing back towards the village. Saw us as God sees us.

We were all running now.

I don't know how long we ran. I remember abandoned shoes, heels stuck in the soft ground and pulled from our flying feet. I remember stockings torn and knees grazed. I remember not caring. I remember none of us caring. For the first time, none of us caring. Because for the first time we thought about something other than our clothes, our looks, our posture. We thought about something more than future husbands and how to impress at a dinner party. But by then it was too late.

The wind's uplift had lost its grasp on the balloon and it was dropping. The basket, no longer a speck against the May sky, grew larger and larger until it seemed only just out of reach. The boy's feet, loose at the ankles, were skimming the grass. His knees buckled to meet the ground. But the wind was still stronger than the anchor of the boy's body and he dragged, first his trousers then his skin tearing on the dank earth.

The balloon, as if sensing its imminent collapse, seized a final chance for freedom. It rose once more and for a moment the boy hung, hanged, in the air below the basket. His arms swung limp at his sides, hands barely poking out from the sleeves of the over-sized over-coat we knew so well. His chin slumped into his chest; his neck encircled by the thick tethering rope that held him.

And then we could see his face. The face that we had studied, discussed, analysed and longed for. The face that Meliss had once joked, as we set off on yet another make-believe errand into the village in the hope of catching sight of him, was 'the face that launched a thousand trips'. We saw his eyes, opened wide the way eyes open only if you are choking. We saw the smeared lines of dried blood which had leaked from his ears, his nose and mouth. His mouth hung open as it never had in life, newly slack-jawed, tongue lolling just inside his lower lip.

As we ran, we hoped it was not him. Hoped it was another, a stranger from another village, another town. We ran, not to his aid, for even to our untrained eyes, the boy was beyond that. We ran to disprove to ourselves that it was him. But we knew then, as his body soared angelic above us. We knew then as we felt the wind drop and saw the body fall. We knew as he hit the ground and crumpled. We knew as we heard the silence of his mother drawing breath. And we knew as we heard her release it. Her cry came from somewhere deep: beneath her throat; beneath her lungs; beneath her heart. It seemed to come, not from her mouth but from her pores. We knew as we heard her scream the last word she would ever speak. His name. Étienne.

Above us, high above the sinking balloon, a large bird circled.

*

But I have jumped ahead as I always do and as I did then, beneath the gendarme's stare, sharp as it was under the interview room's strip lights. He had removed his starched officer's cap and his eyes peered at me, unshielded from the glare. Too frightened by the anger I saw in his thick eyebrows which burrowed into his frown, I did not cry. The crying came later, stifled sobs after lights-out and communal weeping in those last limping classes when the tears rolling down one face would spread and infect us all. 'It is not ladylike,' said Madame in disgust. 'Even you English forget your stiff upper lip'. She was repelled by our tearful presence. She must have longed to see us go. Each teenage face reminding her of what had happened, what we had done.

I told the gendarme of all the beginnings and all the middles I knew. I talked and talked, trying to purge myself of what had happened, what I had done. In my hand, I clasped Étienne's handkerchief, embroidered with his father's monogram: W.S. Walter Stäger, Étienne once told me, was the fastest skier on the mountain. He could do the Grand Slalom in under two minutes and would have gone to the 1948 St Moritz Olympics had he not been run over by one of the first cars to make it into the mountains. 'Owned by a guest at the Palace Hotel of course,' Étienne said. Now Monsieur Stäger was nothing more than blue stitches on white cotton and his son was nothing more than a name stamped across a police file. I pressed the handkerchief hard into my hand as I talked.

I told the gendarme about Madame and Monsieur and the

teachers; I told him about Toinette. I told him about us, the girls. The officer knew us all by now. We were witnesses, *témoins*. Some of us were suspects, though suspected of what we were not quite sure. Our names appeared in the officer's notebook and could probably be heard in the bureaux and corridors of the gendarmerie. Our fingerprints nestled in filing cabinets and our passports, for that week at least, lay in the police safe alongside sealed paper bags containing evidence from other crimes: a forged cheque; someone's stash of marijuana; a knife.

When I left the gendarmerie that evening, I heard a junior officer at the front desk referring to us collectively, as the village boys did, as *les paons*. The peacocks.

*

Even from this distance in time I cannot be sure when it started. Sometimes I think it was the moment Étienne first caught sight of Pen, though she would still have been Penelope then. He was sitting at his usual table in La Scie, fingers skimming the rims of a line of wine glasses filled with different levels of water. As she entered, we saw his fingers waver, suspended in the air like a pianist about to perform a glissando. The hum from the glasses dwindled. He blinked and the ringing resonated again. It must have been less than a second. But we saw.

Other times I think it was before. Getting lost in the Gare du Nord before a ticket inspector who showed me, wet-faced, how to *compost* my ticket and pointed me to the platform. Or Madame telling me to hide my one suitcase under the bed before the other girls arrived with their steamer trunks. Stencilled initials and gold monograms on understated brown leather, fresh from cruises or, I imagined, the Orient Express.

Or was it further back still? The house on Hillcroft Way. The day the letter arrived in its thick cream envelope with Madame's looping French script and the unfamiliar stamp, a violet etching of a chateau on the shore of a mountain lake over the word 'Helvetia'. For it was then that I first heard of Madame, of the Institut Montagnette and, I suppose, it was the first time I had ever thought of Switzerland.

What Jack Did

J.K. Benecke

'Vi *can't* let de *sy*stem be ab*use*d in dis *vay*,' said Mrs Å the Biology teacher.
'You're *right*, it's *get*ting abs*urd*. *Pay*-giz and *pay*-giz of *rubb*ish. Pure *rubb*ish,' said Mrs Ä, the other Biology teacher, waving the yearbook around. Or maybe that was Mrs Å? Jack could never remember which was which. Their surnames were Äckelberg and Åderbrock. Or Åderberg and Äckelbrock. Something along those lines. They both had short grey hair, dumpy figures, ruddy complexions and loud voices. Anyone who thought that all Swedish women were swimsuit models should take a long hard look at Mrs Ä and Mrs Å.
'Pure *rubb*ish!' agreed the one who was not waving the book around, reaching for the biscuits in the centre of the large round imitation-pine table.
Could rubbish be pure? Jack wondered silently before another voice, American this time, intruded on his thoughts.
'Mm, uhh, I think you're right. There do seem to be, well, a lot of pages that, uhh, I don't think can be, mm, really, uhh, justified.' This was Hugo Horne: young, unqualified and new to the school. Carl Gustavs Gymnasieskola – a state school – had, up until three years previously, been the only upper secondary in Stockholm offering full tuition in English. Then the fee-paying, so-called 'free school', English International School Stockholm had launched a rival programme. Able to offer better salaries and incentives, many teachers from Carl Gustavs had been lured to EISS, leaving CGG's headmaster to scrape the barrel of jobcentres to find the native English speakers promised in the school's prospectus. The result was that a handful of surprised Americans and Antipodeans in Sweden for love or other reasons, found themselves swapping bartending or waitressing for teaching sixteen to nineteen-year-olds English, Sociology, P.E., History, Maths, Psychology, or one of the other compulsory subjects in the broad Swedish curriculum (which, in Jack's opinion, erroneously favoured a smattering of knowledge in many fields over in-depth specialisation).

Mr Horne, who had been working in a café and taking a few short courses at Stockholm's university, now taught History and English at CGG. He had a deliberately earnest demeanour which irritated Jack, who seemed to be the only person who realised that it concealed not studious intellect, but ineptitude. Mr Horne either wore his dark bushy hair in a ponytail or let it fall around his face in a protective curtain behind which his round glasses glinted timidly. Today was a curtain day.

'*Great* point, Hugo,' cooed Mrs Einarsson protectively. She leaned over to pat Mr Horne's arm with her leathery hand. Her long fuchsia talons grazed his denim shirt. Mr Horne tipped his head forward slightly, so that his hair concealed even more of his face, and gradually shifted his scrawny body away from Mrs Einarsson.

Jack was trying to imagine that he was elsewhere, anywhere rather than in the Boardroom. But letting his mind wander freely down memory lane was not a good idea. He was safer here, surrounded by people who did not matter.

The room was situated in the school's 'lower bottom' – Swedish for basement – and had white walls, high ceilings and slivers of window set so far up that you could not see out of them. The effect was that of a day room in a mental asylum. The caretakers did not have a ladder long enough to reach the windows, so they were never opened, and the air was permanently musty. Today the central heating was on full blast to combat the November chill, adding the smell of baked teacher to the recycled air.

It had not always been a Boardroom, it used to be a plain meeting room before some misguided corporate jargon had renamed it. Someone, in a fit of wit, had blacked out the A on the plastic sign drilled into the door and squeezed an emaciated E after the R. Probably a student. Maybe not. Meeting room, Boardroom, it was all the same to Jack: boredom.

'*I* tink de first criteria *has* to be at *least* six *monts* of high *profile* ac*tiv*ity around de *school*,' said a very new, very young female teacher who Jack had recently mistaken for a student in a rather embarrassing incident involving the tea and coffee facilities in the staffroom. Today he noticed that she had visibly erect nipples attached to small, pert breasts and did not appear to be wearing a bra under her white v-necked t-shirt (which she had no doubt purchased at H&M. You did not want to get Jack started on 'H&M and its Impact on the Homogenisation of the Swedish Dress Code', one of many faux PhD titles he liked to bandy about).

'Criterion,' he murmured.

'What was that?' Fiona Börjesson, who thought she was his ally, held up a hand in a shushing gesture. A wave of pleasure swept through him. All the faces around the table were turned towards him. He was their Gandalf. No, he was younger than that: their King Arthur, their Aslan, their Jesus. He stopped himself: that way madness lay. He retracted, he was not their Jesus.

'I was just wondering,' he took his time formulating the sentence, pausing to decant more coffee into his mug from one of the flasks on the table and letting the full timbre of his unsullied accent wash over his audience, 'whether we really need to have a yearbook at all. It's an administrative nightmare and now that all the students seem to be immortalising themselves on the Internet, socialising in the ether – beaming their images into space for all I know – it seems a bit redundant.'

Polite laughter ensued, diluted by cries of, 'Well exactly! Quite, quite. Serve them jolly well right if we did scrap it, eh?'

These interjections all issued from Mr Hansson, the biologically one hundred percent Swedish, but emotionally one hundred percent anglophilic Psychology teacher whose tweed suits annoyed Jack almost as much as an H&M wardrobe did. Mr Hansson was in his early 30s and sometimes wore a cravat. His efforts to emulate the speech of an English gent from the 1920s were generally considered successful by the other teachers. Unlike Jack, they had not grown up listening to the BBC radio announcers of the 1950s and so they did not find Mr Hansson's spittle-filled *th*'s, over-emphasised *h*'s and misinterpreted phrases galling. He had a habit of approaching Jack from behind and booming, 'I say, how's this cricket?' 'What what!' or, worst of all, 'Pip pip, sonny bean!' Jack was trying to train his body not to jump when this happened.

The discussion resumed as if Jack had never spoken. He fumed silently and refused to catch Fiona Börjesson's eye even though she kept shooting him conspiratorial eyebrow lifts. He was not their Arthur. They humoured him and pretended deference to his age and nationality, but ultimately they ignored his suggestions. What did it matter how many phoney groups suddenly materialised in time for yearbook photos? Let them all be photographed and photographed and photographed again. The more time the students spent being photographed, the less time they would spend in his classroom.

Last year had spawned: the Piercings Club (two members), the I Look Good Naked Club (seven female members wearing bikinis, five male members wearing thongs barely covering their members), the Asian Vegetarians Club (five members, two of them Asian), the Jews on Wheels group (three members, three bicycles) and the Pony Club. The latter picture showed five boys crouching on all fours. They wore white vests, baggy blue jeans revealing the make of their underwear, and satisfied smirks. On each of their backs sat a girl. The five girls looked as though they could be sisters; each sported long straight blonde hair, a thin body and breasts pushed up to earring latitudes. These Penthouse visions wore jodhpurs and cropped tops. They looked happy.

Jack privately guessed that the photo also made a lot of frustrated middle-aged fathers happy when leafing through their children's yearbook. Though possibly not the fathers of the Pony Club girls. Except for the really sick ones, like Caroline Stallbäck's dad who had recently been convicted of three acts of child molestation, two of which had been carried out on Caroline's little sister. Fiona Börjesson had been outraged when Mr Stallbäck was sentenced to a mere two years in prison – though she simultaneously insisted that 'locking people up is pointless and inhumane' – and had suggested that Caroline should not have to do any homework for the rest of the year 'to give her time to deal and heal'.

When Fiona had asked him what he was going to do to help Caroline, Jack had pointedly remarked that the high profile case (Mr Stallbäck was a well-known lawyer) did not seem to have done the girl's modelling career any harm. You could not pass a 7-Eleven without seeing her bikini-clad body gracing a magazine. 'But it's a question of empathetic healing – ' Fiona had begun to say when Jack shoved his tongue in her mouth and pushed her against the photocopier.

It now occurred to Jack that this incident had taken place more than a month ago and that he and Fiona had not had sex since. This was odd. Their agreement – he would not dignify it with the word 'affair' – was long-standing and driven mainly by Fiona. He glanced at her now, taking in her cropped black hair studded with silvery grey, and the outline of her sagging breasts – she did not believe in bras – under her beige smock thing. Tunic, he remembered, she called it a tunic. She caught his eye and broke into her toothy grin; she certainly did not seem angry with him. Maybe it had not been a month since their Stallbäck conversation. Time moved slowly during a Swedish winter. It was moving exceptionally slowly this evening.

Ban the groups, allow the groups, Jack was beyond caring. He just wanted the meeting to end. He wanted out of the Boredroom, out of this white-walled cuboid which made him think of the beetles he had collected in shoeboxes as a child. Now he understood why they never lived for very long, climbing the walls in a suddenly rectangular world. Hell is other beetles. He felt a squeeze of panic in his chest. He needed to look out of a window, needed to be in a place with a better oxygen-to-carbon-dioxide ratio. The teacher with the pert breasts who did not know the singular of criteria was talking again in her competent but heavily accented English. Her dark red lipstick had smudged slightly, adding a blood-like quality to her butchered syllables. It was strange the way some people could not eradicate the singsong Swedish intonation however hard they tried, creating a vaguely surprised sounding English in which V's and W's frequently swapped places. Hell is other teachers.

'*I* tink dat it's wery im*po*rtant dat ve don't *a*lienate any *stu*dents.'

He felt a wave of irritation rise inside him. He remembered how cheery he had found that Scandinavian rolling speech with its peaks and troughs when he first met Gunilla. She had lit up the dreary London pub on the Holloway Road with her enthusiastic vowels (or 'wovels' as she called them) and exotic demotic. Having lived with it for almost a quarter of a century, however, the cheeriness had become inanity.

The Holloway Road. He tried to stop his mind from heading down that memory lane, but it was too late. He felt the familiar blend of sadness and nausea lurch up through his torso and into his throat. For a second he thought he might vomit. The harsh strip lighting of the Boredroom stung his eyes. He closed them and the emotions withdrew back into the lump in his stomach where they usually lived. He opened his eyes, focused his energies on a large grey smudge on the wall behind Mr Hansson and forced the lid back on his internal jack-in-the-box.

Aboard a White Ship

Rebecca Mackenzie

The East China Sea: 1945

My name is Henrietta S Robertson. That's my English name. It is the name on my nametags, my holiday suitcase and on my cabin-trunk. It is the name written by my mother on the first page of my bible. My Chinese name is Ming-Mae which means Bright and Beautiful. It isn't labelled anywhere. It's just a name I carry in my thoughts, a name that echoes when I try to remember Mother's voice.

Growing up in China, we missionary children have two names. We are called by our Chinese name every day until we are six, when we're sent to the mission's school, high up on a mountain peak. There, answering roll call and following the trail of labels above sinks and hooks and beds, we become our English name. Our Chinese name, like the sound of our mother's voice, fades from memory only to emerge a moon behind a cloud on homesick nights.

I was born blonde and pale as can be. The third of my mother's children, I was the first to survive. When I grew sturdy enough, Mother took me on her visiting trips. She'd place me upon Good News, our family mule, while she, dressed in her blue peasant's tunic, walked along the red dust road, shading us both under a great oiled paper umbrella. Arriving at a village, Mother's work was to visit the women, squatting with them by their black sooted stoves, or sipping tea on a warm brick k'ang. As she spoke, Mother would grip the back of my tunic with one hand, and in the other, she held her gospel. Mother's gospel wasn't a bible or a tract. It was a glove. Each finger was a different colour, black for sin, red for blood, white for holiness, yellow for heaven, each telling a different part of the story.

'Women of Ping-xia village,' said mother, wiggling a finger. 'Do you remember what red is for?' But the women of Ping-xia were more interested in pinching my white skin pink than remembering the blood of Jesus. As I squirmed across the k'ang, tiger faced slippers kicking furiously, mother would say, 'Please ladies, listen to this gospel. It's a matter of eternal life.' She'd wiggle the yellow finger and add, carelessly, for that's how best to begin a bargain, 'Look, Celestial

Heaven.' But the ladies would not look, for tug, tug, tug, they wished to pull my strange white hair. 'It's a ghost-girl,' they said, shuddering, before reaching out their hands to touch me once again. These women know ghost-girls well for they are what float beyond the outer wall of every Chinese village. Some nights when undressing me in the flicker of the oil lamp, mother found string and paper gods in my pockets, placed by the women to protect me from becoming such a creature.

*

I am writing this on the P&O Poona, a white ship that floats across the sea, from Shanghai to Southampton and all the latitudes in between. I am fifteen years old. I wonder if I might be heartbroken. I am lying in my bed which is an army hammock in the Women's Partition. All about there is a strange bunting of stockings and brassieres. The women hang heavy in their swaying beds. Miss Preedy. Miss McArthur. Mrs Roy. We are being repatriated. The war has come to an end, the Japanese camp is dismantled, our mountain school forever closed. Churches are burning all the way up the West Coast. The Reds have come and the missionaries must go. 'Ah ruins, they are a call to faith,' mutters Mrs Roy over her knitting. I have never seen Miss Preedy so still. There are no lines of children to organize, no Evening Prayer to prepare. She's gone a whole day without saying 'Chop, chop'. There is nothing to do but to lie down in a hammock and think of what has gone, of what will come. We are in between places. A pilgrim people. Just as Ruth left Moab and Sarah left Haran, and Noah's wife found herself in a zoo, afloat.

I have decided to write down my own story. I swapped the cigarettes given to me by that American soldier with Mr Gunn and got this Red Cross paper. Mrs Mitchell donated some old sheets of Mozart music that the orchestra played in camp. Miss Preedy, who has asked me to call her Janet, let me use her pencil. Thank you, Janet.

This is a list of what I own. One blue dress, one yellow dress, two pairs of Red Cross pants, my bible with its pressed hollyhocks, Sergeant Nomata's autograph, a sewing kit and half of Nigel Reynold's stamp collection. They are all in my holiday suitcase. I lack a brassiere.

I also lack China and parents. It has been four days since we sailed out past the junks and the fishing boats to where the Shanghai Bund became a flat line. I write from the waves, where there are no flies, there are no birds. If you were to stand on the Bund and look out to sea, my ship would not be on your horizon. I have vanished from China's sight.

China, land of my birth, I watched you disappear, my chest pressed against the railing, my hair blustered this way and that. I cried and cried and no-one came. I stood past lunch and tea-time and no-one made me go in, for I am no-longer a school girl, and until I am delivered to the pier at Southampton, I am not yet a daughter. Land of my birth, how can the women settle so quickly into their hammocks to knit and repair their socks? I stood steadfast until the stars came out, until the only sound was engine and ocean and my own voice, listing the things I love; watermelon pips, red bean buns, the strange twists of your mountain pines. I am listing you so that I never forget. Could you hear me chanting into the wind? That night I slept with a scrape in my throat.

Home, home, home, it's all they ever talk about here in the Women's Partition. Each day Mrs Roy's accent gets more Yorkshire. 'It'll be nice dear, to be at home,' she keeps saying over the clack of her needles. But how can this England be home? I have never been there. And mother and father, what if they walk right past me on Southampton pier? Their eyes searching but unseeing, shouting to the crowd, 'Where is our daughter, where is our daughter?'

I lack the daughter-words to answer them. How to speak to a mother and a father? I must make a new list. A list of daughter-words.

Last night I was so sick of hearing of this England that I swung in my hammock, singing 'China is home', my voice snaking and shrieking like a love lost Dan. The Women's Partition stiffened and tutted. When my song became sobs, Miss Preedy appeared at the end of my hammock, and asked if I thought I might need a wee prayer. I shook my head. No thank you, Janet.

Instead, I rolled over and thought of my mountain. *I lift mine eyes up to the mountain, where does my help come from.* Oh beautiful mountain, remembering you is prayer. I trace you with my fingers. Up, up the Great Steps, across Drill Court, around the Girls' Building all rambled over with morning glory and passion flowers, over the arched bridge where Livingstone and Carey Stream bubble into each other. Leaf by leaf of our dormitory garden, twist by twist of Pine Needle Path, each of the hundred Great Steps, I count everything, one, two, three, like a good girl brushing her hair before bed.

Lovely Miss Ruthers. Everyone knows she is dying. Something in her stomach and it isn't sea-sickness. 'A Psalm, dear,' she said, as I sat by her bed in Sick Bay. I took her bible in my hands. It was light as a bird. Written inside the front cover was, 'Sarah Ruthers, 1897.' Miss Ruthers didn't say please or thank you and I didn't mind one bit for she's an old missionary who escaped the Boxers and survived two Yellow River shipwrecks. Being read Psalms is her right. 'Psalm Eighty-four,' she said and closed her eyes. *My heart and my flesh rejoice in the living God.* I let my voice get softer, a dusk falling, until her eyes came to stillness under her eyelids, and her breath slid easy under her Red Cross blanket. *Yea, the sparrow hath found her an house.* I love to know people's favourite verses. It's like tip toeing across their soul.

This afternoon I was lying on my tummy, listing China, when Elspeth J West came to my hammock again. She stood there swinging me without even saying hello. I turned to glare when I noticed her goldy eyelashes were damp with tears and her nose, pink. I invited her aboard. She got in, curled up and shook like a squall.

The problem is this: Elspeth J West is simply, plainly, and truly, the wrong size for her parents. She and her brother Frank were reunited with them in Shanghai two weeks ago. They are busy trying to be a family in Family Cabins. Elspeth J West is fourteen and taller than me. Huge. Now that she's a daughter again, she's trying to make herself smaller, more huggable. She is trying to be little, just like the girl her parents once knew. But Elspeth J West is so big and grown and golden, that her parents don't know what to do.

I leant over her, 'Would you like me to pray for you?' She nodded. I prayed a pretty prayer of rainbows and eagles then, like the storm on the Sea of Galilee, the tears of Elspeth J West stopped.

I worry my prayers are prettier than my thoughts.

'Elspeth, a question. How to speak to mothers and fathers? How to be in a family cabin?' Elspeth can only shrug her big, soft shoulders. It's like asking a girl about periods. No-one tells you how it really is and you could never imagine it. Especially that squirming in your tummy, how it's the same feeling as getting a premonition.

There is a mirror in the ladies' bathroom. I've been these past afternoons while the Women's Partition is having its nap. I went to visit my face. I made a list. I was accurate. Hello face. You are blue eyes. Pointy chin. Sharp cheeks. You are what they will see when we arrive in England. Are you Bright? Are you Beautiful?

The face blinked. She looked sad. I couldn't see her future.

Tomorrow, I will take Elspeth to visit the mirror. We must practise our smiles.

*

Father sat on the k'ang with his leather bound bible, heavy as a baby, resting on his lap. The light of the oil lamp flickered across the room. It was the night before I left and we were finishing Family Prayers. Father raised his hands in a blessing over us. He said, 'Just like Abraham and Moses, we are a pilgrim people. We are called across the face of the earth. And now Ming-Mae, you are six, and it is time to begin your own journey.' Father looked at mother. She dipped her head. Pinned on the wall behind them was a cotton sheet. Mother had drawn a map of China on it. Black dots for mission stations, blue dots for villages visited, red dots for the Catholics. Day and night a trail of ants worked their way across it.

While mother packed the last items on the school's list into my trunk, Father read from the school prospectus. He read it to me in his bed-time story voice. The first words were 'Huizhou School has been established so that parents can pursue their calling uninterrupted.' As he read, I leant near, and looked at the pictures. There was a school, white buildings above a black ravine and next to it, a picture of a great bell. A pale girl with blonde pigtails was ringing it. The bell was calling us children to the mountain, and from all the corners of China we would come.

Selected Poems

James Trevelyan

I'd like to tell you

I could sit in silence with you
for hours, so I might

describe the impact
of your eyes; everything

you want me to speak
you steal from my tongue

when ours meet; I'm scared
whatever I say will not mean

enough to you – or too much.
Remember that Woolf

you left outside in the sudden
rain? How the pages

glued and word
clung to word?

Lloyd

Dissolve to: LA, '94 - the present day
  – James Cameron

They gave me a name, and does
that not give me life, more,
at least, than UNIFORMED COP,
NIGHT NURSE or FIRST JOCK,

who may have had more to say,
but no claim to an existence
beyond their scene. I suppose
they forgot me, but I'll not

forget the night a naked
colossus walked into my bar, eyes
steely with intent. A Titan:
Atlas having shrugged the burden

at this Western edge of the earth,
eclipsed now by a different purpose
and fearing no consequences. You'll
remember my 10-GAUGE WINCHESTER

LEVER-ACTION SHOTGUN could
reload by the swing of one strong
arm, and my sunglasses so dark
they'd protect your eyes from the white

light of Judgment Day. But you
may fail to recall – before he took
these from me – that I spoke to
this creature like a brother,

its first lesson in humanity: *I can't
let you take the man's wheels, son.*
He drove off, I sold, moved
up-state, never replaced my gun.

When

        we get closer
    to the coast,
gravity
    works differently

      the stones we throw

  shaped

over millions of years
      hang on the breeze
  for one
    moment
        longer

suggesting a hollowness,
            a hidden
        talent for flight;

    seagulls
    ceaselessly
battle

to stay in the air, and only
      achieve the grace
  of other birds
in their
    swoop
        to a landing site;

and when we race against
the sea to keep our feet,

we lift
        our knees
                higher

than we ever would inland,

and the wet sand we carry
        with us onto the dry

is our
        flickering
              left
        on the coastline

Reading a pigeon

I've seen some scrags in my time,
but the one that found its way in
with the seeds and blossom
that warm summer week
looked remarkably fit:

chest pumped, toes and feet
intact, lifting each in turn
as though the open book
on which it chose to sit
was hot sand;

and I couldn't tell if its orange
eyes were trying to describe fear
or safety or some enormous gap
between; in fact, there was nothing
I could understand

except that it was shaking
all over and teaching blues –
not a return to the first chord
at the thirteenth bar but
a wave's distant debut.

Lune

This is not a river but
a tidal estuary, as I hear
the Hudson is, but the silt

unveiled here by far-
retreating sea speaks
differently of its bond

with water, and with
the disappearing moon
which helps it breathe.

It accepts the deep
footprints of birds
who pluck algae

from its skin, and lets
the sun perform
smoothing miracles

on its puckered
flesh, as it sings
to the surroundings:

I am not a river bed, I am
a river bank, in dialogue
with air. See me glisten.

The Chinese Room

L.E. Peters

The twin boys were eight months old when the English teacher arrived in Shanghai. The first sister's room had been soundproofed and was now a nursery, with mobiles and white towelling baby equipment and two new nurses, one from Malaysia and one from the Philippines. There was a bell which played a dinky rendition of Happy Birthday when the babies woke, and a baby monitor which transmitted their gurgles and wails, as if they were ghost children, across the ground floor and along the mezzanine. Wanda's mother said that new babies were very tiring. She had to supervise their feeds and show the nurses how best to bathe them. The other servants, who might have germs, were not permitted to go into the babies' room. At dinner time, or when there were guests, the nurses would bring the babies out on display, sitting on white towels in the white baby suits with the little mittens which prevented them from scratching their heads and making them bleed. Both nurses, now, would smile like dancers and Wally would recline in their arms like a pampered old man, while Willy would flail his arms and open his eyes wide.

Or the other way around. Wanda had thought that Wally's face was fatter, but now she was not so sure. Her younger sister, Weiran, only ever identified one twin from the other by chance. Both Wally and Willy could laugh, now, and Wanda and Weiran would ask their mother to make them do it, for a treat. She would let Wanda hold a baby in her lap while she sat in front of it and talked in a special voice until its little face twisted. Mai, the housekeeper, could also make the babies laugh, by telling them which brother they were. She would bend towards them with her bottom sticking out and her hands behind her back, and when she said, 'Older brother, older brother,' the baby's face would be in creases.

Weiran had behaved worse than ever since Wally and Willy had arrived. At meal times she took food from other people's plates and bent over the serving dishes until her hair dangled in the soup. She put her bare feet up on the table and chewed with her mouth too full and open. Sometimes Wanda's mother said that Weiran could not close her mouth on her food because at eight, she had wobbly baby teeth, but at other times she spoke sharply through Weiran's giggles. Mai, who had once been Weiran's nurse, would come at the end of the meal to stand by Weiran's chair, grim-faced, and pile noodles on a spoon until the plate was clean. Weiran opened her mouth for the spoon like a baby bird. The third sister wriggled instead of eating, slipping out of her chair to go and look over somebody else's shoulder, and she didn't seem to need to sleep either. She woke Mai, who slept on an unrolled mattress next to her bed, at five. She woke Wanda, too, even though their beds were bordered by curtains like the one which divided their desks in the school room.

These days, Wanda shrieked at Weiran when she woke her, bore the grudge through breakfast and sulked in the car all the way to school. Now that she was eleven, Wanda surfaced from sleep aching and miserable with tiredness, barely resigned to the prospect of another day of school followed by another evening of lessons. She seemed usually to be bored or sweaty, and almost always under duress. It was her parents' aim that, apart from those minutes when Wanda was actually sleeping or ingesting food, she use the long, obsessional hours of childhood in tireless preparation for her future. The household had six languages and each child was training for fluency in three of them, though Wanda teased her mother by saying things in clumsy French and Tagalog. Weiran played the guqin, Wanda the piano and from five o'clock on tutors would appear on the doorstep with scrappy notebooks from which they tore sheets of musical notes, equations and classical poetry. Sometimes their own same subject teachers from school flickered up on the video screen by the door, seeming like different people entirely when they put on house shoes to teach a class of one.

The sisters came to the schoolroom and wriggled and flopped about and never seemed to come top when they were in school. They responded to the schedule in different ways. At the age of thirteen, Wendy, the first sister, had ceased to react to verbal stimulation and concentrated her energies solely on video games. Since by strength of will and long exposure she now appeared immune to prompts, commands, threats and shouting, and since she was now physically taller, larger and stronger than her mother, it was no longer possible to separate her from console and screen. Mr Wu, who had himself been educated in England, decided she should go to a London boarding school. Weiran, the third sister, displayed in the company of individual adults a sympathy that might have led them to suspect her of reading minds. Her tractability, in comparison with her sisters, was almost worrying. But while she was capable of filling a page of her notebook with the miniscule furnishings of a tiny mansion for a happy half-hour, she spent her lessons tenaciously dropping pencils, forgetting poems and relaying in anecdotal summary any fiction she happened to have recently been read. The mansions were inhabited by cartoon girls with ballooning heads and gigantic, piteous eyes.

Wanda, at eleven, had a neat, developed little face, a coincidence of characterful features and baby skin that made her, on first encounter, an attractive child. Brought up under the vulnerable and anxious authority of nannies and maids, and the inflexible supervision of her parents, she was discovered by the household and the school to have an uneven temperament. When told to do something she might quietly and promptly begin, or she might be found ten minutes later claiming amnesia somewhere she should not be, or she might shout insults at you either in your own language or in one you did not speak. Mai made her face a stern mask, the maids pulled humorously rueful expressions, and her mother dealt prompt and awesome retribution. The second sister seemed to be inhabited by both a humble pupil and a spiteful autocrat, and her eyes were overwhelmingly wary. It was true that Wanda felt out of her element in the everyday sensory world, harsh and loud when she surfaced from the comfortable realm of English text on a page. She loved stories by Enid Blyton and her hot, angry little dog, and differed most sharply from Weiran in that she was rarely sentimental.

Weiran wanted to know where the English tutor would sleep. Wanda's mother considered the guest room, between the nursery and the massage room, but thought better of it, because she did not want the English tutor to have to be moved when Mr Wu's parents came to stay. She decided that the tutor would sleep below stairs, on the other side from the maids' quarters, next to her sister. Sally greeted the news that there would be an English girl sharing her bathroom by raising her eyebrows and smiling widely. Wanda and

Weiran knew that when she came home from work Sally's presence in striped shirt and suit trousers somehow filled her wing of the house, playing video games and making phone-calls until very late. Weiran, who was also fond of video games, said that the calls were to Sally's boyfriend.

Their mother and their aunt did not really look alike except when they remembered that their mother also preferred to spend her day in her bedroom, watching the maids and the guards on CCTV. She would let the girls look over her shoulder at the grid of grainy little boxes in which the individual members of the household were lined up in busy little rows. In the guard-house, the guard sat with his feet on the desk, listening to music or texting on his mobile, and next to him, in the kitchen, Mary squatted to scrub the floor. The maids did not take days off, and sometimes it seemed to Wanda as if the CCTV was actually just a video-recording played on a loop, and she felt dizzy, as if her eyes had unfocussed themselves. When they were in the schoolroom, Wanda's mother could see her and Weiran sitting at their desks and answering the teacher, while the cook arrived in the wet kitchen and took her scissors to the sink to cut the feet off a chicken. If Wanda had been an English child she might have seen her mother as a spider whose threads ran across the grey-flagged floors into every corner of the house, and who at the slightest unexpected quiver rushed out to address the trespasser. When Mrs Wu was at home, the maids sometimes climbed into the kitchen cupboard if they wanted to talk or text a friend.

It was their father who told them the most about the English teacher. They asked him questions on Sunday morning when Wanda's dog was being exercised. Their father stood with his arms folded watching the guards, who stood apart in the street and threw each other a tennis ball, while Timmy ran between them, barking and jumping.

'This guy is a heavy-weight,' their father said, nodding at one of the guards. 'The other ones are all feather-weight, but this one is heavy-weight.'

He laughed, but Weiran, who did not understand, lolled against his arm and pleaded for more information.

'She will speak like this,' their father said, making his vowels silly and haughty, 'and she will be ever so proper.'

'How old is she, daddy?' Weiran asked.

'She is sixty-five,' said her father. 'Older than your grandmother. And she is very strict.'

This was strange, because usually their tutors did not look older than Wanda's mother, though none of them was so beautiful. Wanda's father joked that their mother was a CEO too, with subordinates who produced neat beds and clean windows instead of presentations, and dinners instead of conferences. Sometimes, Mrs Wu cooked for the dinners herself, but Mr Wu got annoyed when she told the maid to hold an umbrella over her head as she stood at the outside barbeque.

'My wife is from Malaysia,' he said to their uncle. 'And sometimes she does not understand how things should be done.'

Wanda and Weiran could not talk at bedtime because of Mai but on the way to school they sat in the back and spoke in English.

'Will she play games with us?' Weiran wanted to know.

Wanda gazed at the back of the driver's head and spoke with authority.

'Yes. She has to. Our father paid for her to come on the plane. He is her boss, so that makes us her boss, too.'

'Mary and Martha don't play with us,' said Weiran.

'That is because they have too much work to do,' said Wanda, arching her spine and sliding off the seat until she kicked the water bottles in the pouch in front of her. The driver, whose back was sore from cleaning the pool, stirred but did not turn.

'She won't have anything to do except teach us.'

Edify

Timothy Allsop

An excerpt from Chapter Two

'I'm going to be the next 9/11 bomber.'
Martin put down his pen and made Jason look at him.
'That is not in any way an acceptable thing to say.'
Jason Li laughed.
'The Americans are a bunch of wankers. My dad says so. China is gonna bomb the ass out of it one day soon,' the boy continued, with a shrug.
'Jason, I'm going to stop teaching you if you keep on like that. Now focus on the question.'
On the table in front of them was an A3 sheet of paper with a number of historical sources relating to the end of the Second World War. There were two written sources: the first a diary entry of an emaciated English POW in Burma suffering the effects of dysentery, the second a newspaper article describing the capture of Berlin by the Russians. There was also a photograph source, depicting the charred and desolate remains of Hiroshima after the fatal kiss of Enola Gay. It was this picture which had prompted Jason's anti-American invective, the general line of his argument being that he wanted to blow their fat asses sky high because they were Yankee imperialist scum. This attitude prevailed despite the fact that Jason's father worked for an American bank and that Jason had, as a young child, lived in a palatial apartment in the centre of New York's fashionable and painfully expensive district of Chelsea. His bedroom and study area were also caked in the trinkets of latter-day Americana. A Pixar/Disney Toy Story duvet cover swamped his camp bed, an American LA Lakers basketball net was suckered proudly to his door, and a series of framed Star Wars posters displaying characters from the piss poor prequels lined the wall. The only nod to the boy's Chinese heritage came in the form of house slippers embroidered with a phoenix and dragon entwined in a never-ending battle. A pair had also been found for Martin and occasionally he would peer down at his mismatched

socks, thankful that it was the boy's nanny who'd brought him into the house and not the mother. In fact the mother and father were not at home. The mother was attending an interior design conference in Paris and the boy's father had been in Hong Kong for the past three months. The current Li household consisted of Jason Li and his two Chinese nannies, Su Wen and Hui Ling, who ran around after the boy despite being in their late fifties. Barely fifteen minutes into the lesson Su Wen brought the boy four pork dumplings and a green tea for Martin, bowing and nodding in deference at Martin, because her English was almost non-existent.

'If you were able to kill either Hitler or Stalin, which one would you choose?' Jason asked, pulling at a corner of a dumpling.

'I can't answer that.'

'Why not?'

'Because by answering that question I would make myself into some sort of God.'

'But it's obvious. You kill Hitler, then the war would never have started and everyone could have directed their weapons towards destroying communism.'

'You want to destroy communism?'

'Only Russian communism.'

'And where did China get its communism from?'

'It's completely different.'

'That might well be true, but still it's Russia who tried communist ideology first.'

'My dad says the Russians are a bunch of thugs.'

'What does your dad say about the British?'

'He says you are easy to make money from and that you eat too much cheese. I hate cheese.'

'Your dad has lots of opinions.'

'You smell of cheese.'

'Jason. Get on with the question.'

Every five or six minutes Martin would glance at the clock on his phone. After the first half an hour he went to the bathroom and took his time washing his hands, using as much of the Molton Brown hand wash as he could squeeze out of the bottle, relishing the exotic spicy scent which was such a welcome contrast to the 99p supermarket brand he used at home. After an hour he went to the toilet again but as he stood with his legs spread peeing into the bowl he heard a rattling noise coming from behind him. He looked over his shoulder but it was too late. He saw the lock twisting and then the door bounced open and Jason stepped into the bathroom laughing and waving a pair of open scissors in the vague direction of Martin's crotch.

'Gonna cut your dick off you mother fucker.'

And Martin, horrified, masked his penis as best he could and shouted at the boy to get the hell out of the bathroom. The boy made another lunge at him, and Martin desperately tried to stop himself from peeing everywhere but his bladder had other ideas and drained the last of its contents half in the bowl and half around the floor surrounding the toilet. Martin shouted again and finally the boy gave up and went out. Martin kicked the door shut with his right leg and zipping himself up, turned the lock and lent with his back against the door. What the fuck was he going to do? This would be hard to explain to Denise at the agency. He could see the headlines now: *Young Tutor Seduces Minor in Masochistic Scissor Game.*

He looked at his watch and waited another minute. There were only twenty minutes left and then he could run away and never come back. He half cleaned up the mess he'd made, although he left some drops of his piss on the floor as a kind of protest to the splendour of Jason's wash room. Slowly he unlocked the door, half expecting Jason to jump out and shoot him with a stapler, but when he looked Jason was at his desk and appeared to be working. Martin sat down warily, checking the seat for drawing pins.

'I'm doing the answers,' he said.

'Good. Well carry on.'

Jason worked in silence and Martin realized that the boy was scared that he might tell on him. Martin relaxed a little. He took a sip of the green tea and looked out of the window. On the other side of the road he could see a woman on a roof top terrace trimming a set of plants. The terrace was little more than fifteen square feet yet the woman had squashed no end of plants on to it. There was barely room for a wooden lounger which emerged choking from the greenery. Martin wondered why the fuck she didn't move to the country if she liked plants so much. Her apartment, in that part of the city, would have been worth a ridiculous sum, enough to buy a decent bit of house and garden in the country. Some days he despised Londoners.

Jason finished and Martin checked through the boy's answers and found that they were remarkably good. His written English was far above standard for his age, revealing an easy and elegant prose style, through which he'd expressed some neat insights.

'When are you going to move in?' Jason asked as Martin put on his jacket.

'Move in? I'm not moving in. I'm just here to teach you.'

'But we could play on the computer now I've finished all my work.'

'I don't think your mother would be happy paying me thirty-five quid an hour to play on the computer with you.'

'We don't need to tell her. She's away and never comes up here anyway.'

'Well maybe some other time. I have another appointment to go to.'

'You teach other kids?'

'Yes.'

Jason didn't seem to like the fact that he was sharing Martin with other children.

'When are you coming next?'

'I'm supposed to come again next week, but I need to speak to your mother first.'

Martin did not want to commit himself to teaching a child that was potentially capable of cutting off his manhood.

'You have to come again.'

The boy sounded contrite and his pleading almost touched Martin. He wondered how many teachers Jason had been through. For a moment he saw the bodies of a physics and music teacher stuffed into the boy's closet, rotting between old toys. Martin still found it hard to understand how a child grew up in the middle of a city. For him childhood belonged to the countryside, to his own agonizingly nostalgic memories, when going to see friends meant clambering aboard a bike and peddling along ancient country lanes to the next village. He remembered how he, Richard and Ben had often cycled their way to a scrap of private woodland. Once there they would light fires, cook cheap burgers and shoot gat guns at the special needs kid, who used to tag along with them because he had no friends of his own. Martin couldn't remember the name of the kid. All he could recall was that he had the reading age of a six year old and that he attended a special school in town. Then he remembered that he and Richard had played around with one another at Richard's house while his mother was out working late shifts in the local town's launderette. He could recall Richard showing him a series of near naked women he'd taped to the inside of his wardrobe doors. They were all of them topless and lounging over motorbikes and other über-masculine paraphernalia. He thought it funny that Richard should show him these pictures just before the two of them sucked one another off, as though he were reminding Martin that he was very much a heterosexual boy who just wanted to get his end away.

Jason made one last attempt to prevent Martin from leaving by running down in front of him and picking up his shoes. Martin did not bother to chase him upstairs but instead calmly went to Hui Ling and asked if she could fetch them. The nanny wearily called to the boy who eventually returned, handing Martin one shoe at a time. Martin sat on a chair in the kitchen forcing his feet into the shoes, while Su Wen, barely aware of his presence, set about preparing the boy's tea.

'When is Mrs Li back?' Martin asked.

'Mrs Li not here this week,' Hui Ling replied. 'You need speak with her?'

'Yes, but I can phone her.'

'You leave message?'

'No, it's fine.'

'He a good boy really,' Hui Ling said, as though this was an oft disputed subject.

'Yes, well goodbye.'

Martin stepped outside and as he walked down the path Jason came running out after him.

'Goodbye,' the boy shouted, forming his arms into a Heil Hitler gesture.

Martin winced and looked around to check no-one was on the street. Then he turned and walked away without saying goodbye.

Faringdon Park

Annabel Banks

From Chapter One

Getting the bike upstairs and into the flat makes you want to scream. The heave-and-bump is tricky; all the weight is at the back of the frame, but the handlebar twists in a confusion of cables and, as you fumble in the shadows, the pedal ticks round to stab that dirty spot. Bang. Every day the same place, back of the heel, spiked metal and strained tendon coming together in a moment of lip-biting agony, but you can't rub it or you'll drop the bloody bastard thing.

You shut your eyes. One held breath, and the pain becomes payment for the safe ride that so often swings past rain-blurred messages taped to fences, browning flowers scattered on mud. In some part of your mind, Di lifts a shoulder. *Ride on the pavement,* that's what she means. *There are old cyclists, and there are bold cyclists, but there are no –*

Lift from the frame, shoulders and back solid, thigh-muscles warm, and hold another breath for the last ten seconds as you follow up the line of wear in the carpet. Soil-edged steps, oil-smudged walls. Home, in all its garish glory. Home safe, the roundabouts beaten once more.

Tomorrow you'll remember lights. Tomorrow you'll wear the helmet. Cross heart and hope to –

'Cass?'

Summer is calling you. She must be back early, fixing her usual snack. There's a smell of burnt toast in the hallway. 'Man cannot live on bread alone, but Flora and ketchup makes it a meal,' she told you the first time you saw her eat slices of red bread. You kick off your steelies and wrench at the fleece, fluff over your mouth, against your lips.

'Cass?'

You haven't undone the button again. It catches your nose, scratches your forehead.

'Cassandra?' She holds the last syllable, a swooping note that shakes like a singer on tv. You want to laugh, not just because it sounds funny. One day you'll tell her your real name. Miss C on the bank statements. Passport in the drawer.

'What?'

'I'm in your room. Don't kill me.'

Getting into your room is tricky, too. Strategic jumps between dresses and jeans, makeup, straighteners, piles of junk where you've emptied your pockets after work: washers and nuts, scraps of metal, rusty plasters. The tiny window is open but the air still smells like perfume, WD40, ashtrays.

Summer is standing with her hands behind her back, hiding the long nails, the elaborate designs in yellow and green. 'I'm just looking for the bottle opener.' She toes a coffee-stained magazine. 'See it?'

You don't like people going in your room. Not only because of the mess – Summer's room has the odd mouldy cup and pile of unsorted laundry – but you can't help feeling that it gives too much away, or rather shows what isn't there. The bottle opener is by the bed, corkscrew wound into a pot of kiwi-fruit lip balm. You think about the sharp coil of metal, about using it to carve KEEP OUT into the wood of the door, or, even better, the skin of your forehead.

Instead, you use your t-shirt to wipe away the green grease and pass the tool to her, handle first. 'Starting early?'

'Wine in the week numbs the pain. I lost three today and Frog wants to see me at nine.'

You know you should make some sort of noise – at least double check what it was she'd lost three of: clients, appointments, builders or bathroom suites – but you're uncomfortable, scalp and top lip pricking with sweat. You leave Summer to go and splash cold water on your face, which doesn't help much; the heat is inside, a chemical fire that needs a blue-banded extinguisher, not a red-banded one. Pull the tab back, hold firm and depress, avoiding eyeliner, eye shadow, mascara.

When you return, damp, pink, you see Summer has poured you a glass of the strawberry-flavoured rosé she prefers and left it on the scarred and wobbly coffee table. The bottle is in the kitchen, you can see it through the hatch. The threads of the screw-cap glisten.

The man who shouldn't be living below you turns the radio on. The Radio One DJ is laughing; the same voice that soundtracked your last hour in the zone, followed you to the toilets, the clocking-out machine, the bike shed.

'Bloody hell.' A song begins, one they've played five times already. The bass thumps circles into the surface of the wine. 'It's like he waits for me.'

Summer stamps her foot. Not too hard. 'I can hear him snoring at night. He must sleep right under my room.'

'That means he can hear you, too.' You make a farting noise, tongue out, eyes round, then realise you've missed an opportunity to tease her about sex. 'Ooh Rob.'

'Don't.' Her hands are to her face, over her mouth, talons spread. She could be laughing. 'When's he leaving?'

'Never. Every time the landlord looks he's melted into the walls.'

'He's Batman.'

'More like the Joker with that face.'

You are pleased with this comment. At work the guys talk in a code of name-calling; requests for maintenance or pallets of material wrapped in unflattering comparisons, doubts about sexual prowess or mental capacity. When you first temped in A-Building, loading the front of a welding robot with odd shapes of metal, you thought it was spite, or at best, a gallows humour cultivated to get through a hard day. Now you recognise the game, kicking words like footballs round the shop floor.

It was a hard code to crack. At first your sex bent the banter away, like light through a prism. But you listened and contributed the odd comment over the onslaught of radio, whirrs of the robot motors, controlled explosions of the spot-welding guns, and you laughed when the boys laughed, got quick of tongue as well as hand, loading the welders, the nutters, the guns. Got mocked, but gently. Fitted in.

Di shakes her head. *Almost.*

'Let's go down and tell him to shut the fuck up.' There is no way Summer would ever say this. Her call-centre voice is too sweet, too young-girly to swear convincingly, and she knows it. She's better at cajoling, wheedling for what she wants. She got the landlord to change the shower head and paint her room with one phone call. You were lying on your sofa, listening. She almost lisped.

88

'Yeah.' You don't want to. The wine is cold and sweet. 'Or we could write to Mr Owens again.'

'We've done that. Let's go down. Be brave.' She looks for a word. 'Feminist.'

That's funny. 'Go on then, Germaine.'

'Come with me.' She tops up your glass. 'How scary can he be?'

'He doesn't look scary. He looks like a mechanic. Overalls and roll-ups.'

'Well then. Bring yours and you can smoke together. Talk about machinery. Find common ground.' She has your wrist now and is pulling. You lift yourself slightly on your thighs to give her some help; if her hand slipped she'd hit the wall, hard. 'Don't make me beat you up.'

You stand and look at the bird-bones of her throat. Summer is small. Her curls are bigger than her head.

'Alright.' But the moment you say this, the radio switches off. The room is silent except for the rattle of magpies, a sound blown over from the park.

'Maybe he's going out. We could catch him.' She hasn't let you go, pulls you over to the window. You think about twisting from her grip, going to your room, locking the door.

It's not that you don't like her. It's not that.

You pull back the mismatched curtains and look down to the garage forecourt. Car innards litter the concrete over an oil-stain that spreads in the shape of a question mark. Someone is moving around right below you, but you'd have to lean out of the window in order to see them properly and the window only opens about six inches. All you can see is the corner of a red shoulder bag.

'We can't go down now. Someone's there.'

As you say this the girl takes a few steps back, and you can see her hair, bleached bright and brittle, an inch of dark root slashed across her skull. There's something wrong with her hand, a malformed mass of angry pink. Maybe she's been burnt.

'Who is it?' Summer is next to you, trying to squeeze her head out of the window. She has spoken too loudly and the girl looks up, frowns, looks away, still talking. You step back from the window in panic.

'She saw me.'

'So? You're allowed to look out of your own window.'

Yeah. You pull the curtain again and see that it's not her hand but the thing she is holding that is pink and fluffy, like a toy, but she's too old for toys: eighteen, perhaps twenty. Maybe she's got a kid. She's talking through the concertinaed metal doors that are separate the forecourt from the workshop, and she must have leant on a shutter because you hear the boom and squeak of them shifting over her high voice. Something about the cadence, the length of the sentences between breaths. Not from round here.

'Let's go down while she's bending his ear.' Summer's hand is back on your arm. 'He's less likely to get shitty with an audience.'

'The music's stopped.'

'It'll start again.'

Probably. You should go down, but what should you say? *Excuse me but we were wondering... Listen, you wanker...*

You turn on the television, sink into the sofa and reach for the remote, deciding to change the subject. 'Rob over tonight?'

'We're having some selfish time.'

That again. 'How long for?'

She smiles, but it's just lips moving. 'I reckon he'll be here before I've finished my toast.'

You hum a neutral response and lie back, overcome with tiredness. The wine, the complaining, the twist in your stomach from being caught spying – her frown had hurt you, why had it hurt you? – all force you back down onto the cushion. You close your eyes and listen to the magpies, to the up-and-down of the girl's voice, the sounds of metal on metal.

It's a calm time, after the bike's up the stairs and the blood has left your cheeks; knuckles and thighs loosen, lungs feel clear. The ride takes thirty-five minutes, but you only remember five, when the side of the railway bank drops away and the sky opens before you. Today apricot and lilac clouds, cut by plane trails, parcelled themselves into regular chunks, with only the John Murray building, that odd tower in the shopping centre, tall enough to pierce the view.

If you were ever going to jump you'd get up there, to tumble from the top and splash the pedestrianised area. It would be quick, even though it's a long way down; a rush of wind in the ears, a wet stain between chewing gum and bits of cheeseburger. The rising John Murray means you are minutes from home, a short push left and work is truly done for the day, but it always saddens you to see it: a raised middle finger, telling the sky to fuck off.

Selected Poems

Christian Ward

The Real Red Riding Hood

Everything you've read about me is a lie:
I detest the colour red, look away
at the sight of ketchup, traffic lights
and post boxes. I like the colour blue.

Or yellow. Yellow's good. The old woman?
I visit my Nan, who runs a B&B in Hastings,
come back stinking of the sea and vinegar.
Pets? I once befriended a fox in my garden,

fed it greenish strips of bacon studded
with bluebottles. Didn't seem to mind.
But a fox isn't exactly a wolf, is it now?
And reports of footage of me on the internet?

Those costumes aren't mine. I know nothing
about special effects or make-up. I can't
do impressions; have never been to a wood.
Listen, my name is Dave. I work in an office.

Girl on the District Line

Reach into her eyes
and you might scoop
a handful of koi

turning the carriage
walls gold and orange;
a smattering of lily

pads, frogs, water
boatmen and sticklebacks.
If you're lucky, a heron
still at the water's edge.

Teleshopping

This isn't a channel I've come
across before: the presenters
are selling Idi Amin's head
(throwing in Stalin's liver),
Ceauşescu's feet, Mussolini's
belly. Saddam's heart, a recent
acquisition, thumps to lounge
music in its jar. Free P & P
if you order before midnight.
General Franco's lips, a bargain
at £99.99. I buy them as a talking
point for parties.

Fascinated by these oddities, I check
daily to see their latest offerings:
Tito's nose, a wig of Antonescu's red
hair. Salazar's ears. The suddenness
of sirens. A transparent crate
brought in: Nero's testicles, black
as volcanic ash. I remember
learning how he tried to turn his lover,
Sporus, into a girl and check my Adam's
apple, rummage around my underwear.
General Franco's lips curl into a grin
as my wife erupts, starts to smoke.

Filming 'The Beheading of Daniel Pearl'

Week twelve. The special effects
guy has quit, citing 'insensitive
subject matter'. Asshole. $300k
down. Maryland is no Pakistan

but between the minaret-necked
cormorants and hillbilly locals
I can't tell the difference. Week
eighteen. The walk-on playing

Pearl's Taliban executioner can't
hold the replica scimitar steady,
doesn't believe it won't cut. I press
the edge against my right arm, point

to the dent, shallow as a GI's crew-cut,
it leaves. $500k down. The man
is still shaking. Dick. Week twenty four.
Some pathetic loser has left a fake head

drooling ketchup outside my trailer. $2m
Down. My head is already loosening itself
from the neck. I don't need a gimmick to tell me
this is the worst death I've experienced yet.

Spock

He's the ideal flatmate: clean, tidy,
never drinks or smokes. Doesn't get music
but that's okay. I've learnt to stop staring
at his ears in case he grips my neck
and I collapse like laundry on the floor.
Some days, late at night, I hear him muttering
'Captain, Captain, Captain' into a shoe
and laugh to myself. Spock, fine as he may be,
doesn't make for the best company. Everything
has to be logical: call centres, mangoes, even *sex*.
My girlfriend says he's a pervert whenever
she's around, that he leers at her in a strange way,
as if something is trapped under his skin
and he's desperately trying to get rid of it. Weirdo.
And, if you're wondering, never talk to him
about poetry. He bloody hates it. You can almost
smell the dactyls bubbling on his tongue
as he drones on, how illogical it is to describe
emotion on paper, before becoming still
like a heron about to dive into the dark of a pond
it's never seen before.

The Butterflies, Kew Gardens

The zebra longwing zooming
past your head to feed
on a piece of papaya held

your attention more than
any conversation with me;
the silence between us

increasing as we walked
through the greenhouse,
past jostling tourists cooing

at the halogen of a holly blue
or rapt by atlas moth cocoons,
expecting a Houdini-like ta-da!

On the train home, something
inside me burst but all I saw over
my shoulder was a pair of black
pinheads and a long proboscis.

The Lives of the Saints

David Gill

The last time Luke had seen his mum had been ten years ago, at least that was the last time he had seen her alive.

She was walking along Church Street, Hackney with two of her girlfriends, drunk, loud, a whirl of colour against shops shuffling customers into an autumn afternoon.

They laughed their way past Clive, his long body propped against a stop sign. He slid a comment through a grin of missing teeth, she raised a finger for him to spin on.

Luke's mum.

She saw him and with a shriek hurried over. Three days since she had been home and she had missed him. She kissed him, leaving a lipstick map of her mouth on his seventeen-year-old cheek.

'On the look for girls,' said her friend Gwen, streak of piss thin, face as weathered as the flat she retreated to when drunk to have it out with God.

'He's got his run of girls.'

His mum's voice, Cardiff, boasting on him, was cigarette smoke and cider and babycham bubbles as she hugged him around the neck.

'He can have his run of me,' encouraged Jenny, her body curves that had never quite gone to fat.

'He's not for you.' Luke's mum placed her small, square form between him and them: 'Meet you at The Crown, I got to spend time with my son.'

'Mother Theresa,' said Jenny, turning.

Mum shook her head: 'She didn't have kids.' Then, to Gwen: 'Leave us a couple of cans.'

Gwen fished two cans of cider out of a carrier bag added a can of beer: 'For the boy,' then arm in arm with Jenny, continued along Church Street toward The Crown.

Luke watched them go, as bright and sweet as the lollipops his mum had smuggled into church. She dragged him along there when she was too sad for anything else.

'Let's sit down.'

She led him to a bench, one of three on a concrete apron set back from the corner of Yoakley Road. The space had a Hackney Council sign: The Levy Memorial Garden. The bench complained as Levy no longer could as it took their weight.

'So, what have you been up to?' She passed him the can of beer.

'Not a lot.'

She lit a cigarette, puffed it once to get it going, handed it to Luke, lit one for herself, opened the cider. 'Been going to school?'

'Or the library.' The library was opposite The Crown, its Victorian grandeur pimped with modern displays. It seemed embarrassed, exhibited like that.

They drank and smoked as the sun slipped under the skirts of the world.

Clive, denied access to the pubs on Church Street, started to shout obscenities and soldier tales from his past and what he was going to do to who and when and how they deserved it. To no-one, just into the air from which the light was bleeding.

'Spaso,' said Luke.

His mother looked at him.

'What? You like him?'

'He's a good man, he's just carrying some damage.'

The last can they shared, mum sipped, Luke sipped. Above them the sky set into constellations.

Nothing changes, he thought.

He said: 'Do you know when we look at the stars we look back in time?' It was something he had learnt from one of the thick books he had borrowed from the library.

'Will you look back at me?' asked mum.

'You'll always be around.'

She smiled her lipsticked smile behind the glow of her cigarette. 'Not for always.'

They watched the stars some more.

*

Luke opened his eyes. His five foot eight frame was laid out on the mattress where he had left it. Clare wasn't alongside him. Through the window of his flat Hackney was pinned up blue.

His mobile was sounding Jar Of Hearts. That was what had

woken him.

He reached for his phone.

'Hello?'

'What are you doing with Rose?'

A thin, angry voice whistled at the end of the line.

'Frank.' Frank tall and lean and apparently back with Rose.

Frank and Rose had been on and off for a couple of years, two nights ago she had assured him they were off, finished, kaput forever. He had wanted to believe her.

Forever had lasted for two days.

He sat up. Frank worked for Charlie and so did he. This needed to be sorted out.

Last night's drink slopped against his skull as he tried to bring the room into focus.

'What are you doing with Rose?' Frank repeated.

'Nothing, I haven't been seeing her.'

The room stabilised into a sink, a gas ring, a door that led to a box of a bathroom.

What had he been drinking?

'The Crown, the night before last.' Frank bore on.

Luke's eyes moved over the familiar, a table, a desk pushed under a window, a chest of drawers in which two of the four drawers were sprung from their runners, a small sofa yellow and battered. His flat.

Concentrate.

'I was drinking, she walked in, what was I supposed to do? Walk out?'

'You've got legs, haven't you?'

He looked at his legs on his grimy red duvet.

'We just ran into each other, it was nothing.'

Rose, her laugh, how he had been caught up in that. Not nothing.

'You had breakfast with her.'

Fuck, he was getting all CSI on him.

'Says who?'

On the carpet lay cans, cigarette stubs, a pizza box. Outside Lordship Road complained about it being another working day.

'Mickey saw you, one of the veggie places on Church Street.'

Mickey was a friend, a bit mental and he couldn't keep his mouth shut.

'I'm not vegetarian.'

'Who is? Wankers. But you were at Le-Gum, one of those places.'

'Mickey doesn't know what day it is half the time. I wasn't at the Blue Legume, I've been taking it slow since Clare.'

The mention of Clare made Frank chortle. 'That girl did a number on you. Still pissed?'

Luke focused on a laptop, next to it a shelf of books, mostly maths.

'I'm taking a break from girls, all of that.'

'So, what, you're gay now?'

'No.'

He focused on *Teach Yourself Algebra*. Top left, the first. The cover showed a boy studiously bent over a book. You couldn't make it out but he had always imagined it was Teach Yourself Algebra. Recursive, like a mathematical joke.

As a kid he had kept checking the book out of the library, in the end he had tucked it into his jacket and walked out without the stamp. The librarian had not looked up. It was just like loaning it.

Him, eight years old, and *Teach Yourself Algebra*.

They were still together.

'You're like Stevie? Up or down?' Frank was still at the gay thing.

'Top or bottom... ' as Stevie in this room had drunkenly explained. Clare had been there, swigging wine from a bottle. First time Luke had met her.

He had said all the right things to Stevie, had been supportive, and Stevie had nodded: yes, you get it, and had started in with the gin.

With Stevie passed out he had tumbled into bed with Clare.

Not like Stevie, she had smiled.

It had been easy and right, like the sums in *Teach Yourself Algebra* it had been forever.

Had he thought that? That was embarrassing.

And now she was gone.

Frank said: 'Jesus, you know the lingo. Top or bottom, legume, vegetarian. How gay is that?'

'Shit, Frank.'

'And Rose? If you're not gay? The Crown, the Blue Le-fuckinggume?'

The books ran from *Teach Yourself Algebra* to *Nash Game Theory*. The current arrangement was chronological.

'You know Mickey, he makes mistakes. There's nothing going on.'

Frank said: 'I'm having lunch with Rose, The New River.'

A pub at the top of Lordship Road.

'Great.' Really: fantastic.

'We should talk.'

Luke closed his eyes. Best if he steered clear of Frank and Rose for a few days, it would give them a chance to bed down. He felt his mouth make a smile at the pun. Dumb, he thought, dumb.

'If you want, Frank.'

'Yeah, I want. One-thirty, the New River.'

Luke heard him sucking breath, pictured thin lips in a long face. The face was furious.

'You know if you touch her, I'll have to kill you.'

'I know that.' The October morning grinned in at him.

'Just so we understand each other,' said Frank and hung up.

Luke dropped the phone. Bloody Frank. Then: Rose, she could have let him know, and remembered her walking in, explaining that Frank had been playing around: 'With Susan fucking O'Halloran, can you believe it?' as though a different girl, a better girl, would be more acceptable but not Suzy fucking O'Halloran. She had taken a stand there. She had been angry, crying angry.

He had shut up and let it happen.

On the table a book was open to Euler's version of the Zeta function. However complicated there were rules and procedures.

This he understood.

He looked at his room. The whole place needed cleaning up.

Time Death

William Fowler

I stop with one hand on the gate and watch him go straight past me.
'Oi,' I say.
Harry turns round. He looks at me and then up at the house and his frown takes on a shade of something like suspicion. The place is nothing special: red-brick with two storeys staring down at us, a privet hedge with a shopping trolley crouching behind, rotten mattress with broken glass caught where it's half-folded against the wall and lot of sticky-looking weeds growing up between the litter. I open the gate and make a gesture like 'After you, Sir.'
Harry looks left and right, a villain's reflex, and then goes up the chequered path to the door, which he immediately starts to rattle, and also gently kick. I come up behind him with the key to the padlock.
'Out the way.'
The lock snicks open and Harry steps round me and is in there, filling the room, occupying the space. His shoulders stretch his Ted's coat, a drape number that he's gone at with scissors, then poured gloss paint on to, the kind used to paint post boxes, actually exactly that kind, stolen from a council depot where he had a few days work. It's all down one side of him, so he looks sort of half-made. He stops in the middle of the hall, blocking me in, so if I wanted to get past I'd have to edge by against the wall. Instead I close the door and wait. The room looks different with him in it. I'm nervous I suppose. I want him to like it.
My preparations have been careful. This room, being where I started, has had more work than some of the others. Like I took a golf club that I found in one of the cupboards upstairs and popped the mirror on the wall. Awwhhhooooooooooopop. Once I'd done the mirror I went over to the banisters. I went at the pommel at the bottom of the rail with the club, denting the pommel, which is the size of a child's head, quite badly and bending the club out of all recognition. Golf, for instance, would be out of the question. Bits, chips of wood lie round about. Splinters. But I had not achieved

my original aim of taking it off altogether and that had upset me, or driven me on you could say, on up the stairs where I'd tried to kick out each of the banisters, one after another. Some had buckled on the end of my toe-capped boot and some had just cracked off, come away at the base. I'd needed both hands to get the necessary purchase so I'd flung the golf club at the window in the door. It's still hanging there actually.

As a finishing touch I dragged some of the clothes down from upstairs. Handfuls of them, from the drawers, and set fire to them on the tiles where there was less chance of the whole place going up. There's an arm of a cardigan, charred and frayed at the end. There are some black marks on the wall where I'd kicked the things against it to put them out, and there's a spicy smell in the air, which is the fragrance of burnt polyester.

The Horse takes all this in. He takes in the wallpaper, which is grey, with a pattern including birds and bamboo with clouds of brown damp on it. He takes in the plasterwork, covered in paint gone off-white and thick as cake icing. The coloured tiles in blue and green. Squares and triangles. He takes all this in, nods and then gobs. He is a most prodigious gobber.

'Nice gaff. This is, I do believe, a nice gaff.'

Harry has this way of talking which is arcane. He imagines himself strutting about, a visible figure in a visible movement, rather than the thing he is which is a conman, a drug-dealer, a bottom feeder. He would be right where he is regardless of the time, find his way like a cockroach finds the dark. He's not even that young, Ruth is twenty-three, twenty-four at the outside, Sue even younger, twenty-six is practically it. And he's not into music he just thinks that the girls are easier and he can shift more drugs around us lot and without recourse to violence because we are younger undernourished types of people. He's a poser really, in his way.

I know this room well and it gives me a strange feeling having the Horse in here. Like the one you get in dreams sometimes, when things come together, two things that you thought you'd never see in one place. Or when you meet someone who you know for a fact to be dead. Not good dreams necessarily.

'The gas and the bog all works does it?'

He's got the light switch, one of those nineteen forties Bakelite ones, between his finger and thumb like a nipple and he flicks it on and off a few times. The bulb flashes weakly in its fitting. A lot of small dead flies are somehow stuck to the wire. Funny I'd never noticed them before.

'Yeah, all mod cons,' I say.

He nods, considers and then gobs.

'What's through here then?' He pushes open the door to the front room.

'Living room.'

I follow him in. There's not much in the way of furniture. Just a threadbare carpet with an armchair and a ruined sofa standing on it. Net curtains on lengths of bamboo across the lower panes of the dirty windows. The old woman put them there on account of the faces that she sometimes saw peering in. I wonder what she would have made of Harry. I imagine shouting into her ear:

'I've brought a friend to stay.'

Her nodding and smiling. Sitting in her chair, shaking among the bottles and talking to people that weren't there. When I bent close enough to hear her, holding my breath against the sour smell of her rotten insides, she'd say that the old man was ignoring her. Pretending to be deaf, she knew his game. Of course the old man was long dead, but when I'd tell her so she'd puff out her cheeks and stare like she'd never heard anything so preposterous.

The Horse goes up to the window and lifts the edge of the curtain to peer out – inspecting the shit in the front garden, nodding to himself some more, like it all means something.

This house is mine now: the walls, the floors and all the spaces between. Even the rugs and the wallpaper they're all mine. It took me a while to realise that I could do what I wanted with them. Then I made a bonfire in the garden of the broken-legged chairs and bedside tables. I took the books from the shelves and threw them out of the window, onto the muddy lawn. You can see them from my room at the top, lying like dead birds with their feathers all over the place. I lobbed bottles over the roofs at the back and listened for the smash. I tore down the curtains. I knifed the settee. And then I thought: 'Now what?'

I couldn't go back to art school. Watching the old hippies trying to poke the little art girlies, confusing them with politics so they could slip them a length, it was just depressing. Teaching us not how to draw, but how to look like we knew how to draw. Waste of time. And like, the state of the world being what it is, like we need more pictures. More studies in charcoal and still lives in oil. I had it all right here anyway. The maggots teeming in the kitchen bin, the flies drawing shapes around the light-fittings. Dust settling on everything. They say it's dead skin don't they? Dead skin and cat hair and we breathe it all day long. Still life.

Disappear Here

Thomas Ogier

From the novel Wake, *a psychological thriller about the hunt for a missing person — a traveller who has disappeared outside a small New Zealand town — narrated by two rival investigators: a lawman, and a journalist.*

DI Morris:

The car was four miles out on the Pig Route. A white metal speck on the huge valley floor, cracked brown hills to the left and right, the pass up ahead used only by trucks that roar past bout one an hour.

Whole thing was full of junk — fishing rods on the front seat, books, a tent in a sack, rotting food, a small tv with no plug, a barbecue in the trunk with a full yellow gas canister attached on a hose. There was a black condom tied to the arial, blowing in the wind. I ask you.

First thing Andrews says, he says, 'Driver's better off out there Morris, better off than in this rusted heap, looks about ready to pop.'

Radioed for the car's history — white Honda, 1985, five-digit number — but for years it'd been handed back and forth from travellers to bums, mostly unofficially for cash. There were unpaid parking fines on her, but nothing named. When I put down the radio I remember Andrews peering through the driver window.

'Well well,' he said, like he'd seen something, then he put his palm on the glass and pushed down, and it slid open.

'Used to have one of these myself,' he tells me. Then he unlocked the doors from inside and let himself in, though he didn't sit, he just leant and looked, turned over bits with plastic gloves and took photos.

Meantime I peered around, but any tracks had been washed away by the rain.

'It's been here a week,' I said. 'Truckies saw it on their way over the pass, then noticed it still here on their way back.'

'Yup,' he said, 'maybe was one of them picked up the driver, whoever he was.'

And that was the way we found it, no sign of a driver, no keys, no tracks, and about a thousand clues inside. We bagged some, till we ran out of sample bags, then returned the next day with the forensic team from the city. They came with big ideas and attracted big news.

...

Sarah Barlow came through the station doors the day after the car photo went in the paper. She was holding it. She was shaking too. Somebody talked to her at reception then called me over but I already knew what it was about, from the sight of her.

'You know whose car that is dear?'

She nodded.

'Can you tell me where they are?'

She shook her head.

'Sergeant, will you please get this young lady a tea and take her to my office.'

She followed him. A willowy, beautiful girl with real long brown hair. Her face red from crying.

She thanked me for the tea and identified John Andrew Swift as the car's owner in the same breath, as though she wanted to get it out before she started sobbing again, which she did.

'I'm sorry,' she said.

'Take your time.'

She said he was English. That he painted. That he was a wild one and they were lovers.

R Ward:

Two weeks later

The CCTV footage showed him standing at the very edge of the rear deck, looking out over the sea. He leant against the rail and barely moved during the first hour of the journey, the strong westerly whipping his clothes and hair against him. He had a brown shoulder bag and wore a dark blue T-shirt and jeans. The meter or so in which he stood was the only portion of the deck still in the evening sun – though it was hard to tell this from the grainy footage – as the rest was shaded by the huge metal stacks of the ferry.

45 minutes into the journey a hulking Maori man wearing shades and a blue chequered jacket, so large that it must have been custom made, walked over and spoke to him. There were four other men and a woman besides, each wearing sunglasses and motorbike gear; patch-strewn leathers, steel-toed boots, bandannas. The large man talked to him for a few minutes, his enormous back to the lens, and then turned, smiled and laughed. Moments later he clapped him on the shoulder with an open hand – an apparently friendly gesture, but one delivered with such force that the 27-year-old stooped forward and grasped the rail.

The video had no sound. Even if it did – I realised as I stood on the rear deck in the exact spot where Swift had stood weeks earlier, my hand on the rail – their voices would have been drowned out by the roaring engines and the howling wind. It chilled my skin and filled my ears, and I wished it would carry to me an echo of the dialogue that had been exchanged there. I ran my fingers along the cold metal bars and imagined his prints in place of mine. Then I dug my hands into my pockets, shivering despite my jacket, the salt spray wetting my face as the boat surged forward.

I'd been able to identify the big Maori soon after seeing the footage, but not to contact him. Carl Hoeft of 17 Hamilton Drive, Manorburn, didn't seem to have a landline, let alone mobile phone or email. It had crossed my mind to give the police his name – anonymously of course – but then they'd get there first, and I would've played a strong card. No, I would find him myself.

Endless blue sea stretched out ahead, its undulating surface sweeping below the bow. Evening sun reflected up off the water and seabirds with curved wings cut through the gale. Perhaps it had been this view that inspired Swift, some weeks after his voyage, to get a tattoo of a gull crossing his torso. It was small enough to be invisible unless sought, a few inches from his naval, a sharp line like an incision.

I had put as much in the first missing person article's factbox

under 'Distinguishing Features; Tattoos or Birthmarks', of which I carried a cutting. It was now two weeks old. I pulled it carefully from between the notebooks and pens in my satchel, drawing my jacket around to provide shelter from the spray:
John Andrew Swift. 27, British.
6 foot 1. Estimated 13 stone.
Blond with brown eyes.
Last seen: Wake, Maniototo, 12 March, 2pm.
Blue shorts, black shirt, flip-flops.
Honda Civic: white with hand-drawn illustrations on panels.
Squint in left eye, tattoo of small black seabird on stomach, burn scarring on right forearm.

There wasn't much to go by, and it had been hard to find photographs. The mugshot on the cutting was particularly useless, an unclear image in which he didn't even look at the lens. I had lifted it from a friend's Facebook account, for Swift didn't have one of his own.

When he made the crossing from Wellington to Picton the sea was calmer than on my subsequent journey. Reports from that day showed that though the wind was up, the swell was low, and his ferry made good time. Mine, on the other hand, departed a full half hour late, before following the same route. Looking past the bow at the horizon I imagined his ship in front of mine, its metal hull chopping through the waves ahead, tipping almost imperceptibly from side to side and leaving a long trail of whitewater in its wake.

I looked around the deck at my fellow passengers. The same mix of tourists, backpackers and businessmen that he would have seen. A 60/40 split of car and foot travellers – foreign youngsters with dreams of finding themselves, their backpacks heavy with guidebooks and half-filled journals, next to middle-aged tour groups destined for whale-watching excursions and guided buses. I wondered how they had looked through Swift's eyes.

Both he and I chose to travel with our own vehicles. My gleaming black Toyota awaited me on the lower car deck, a few rows from where his rusted Honda was once parked. Before coming above I hid for some time in the ship's groaning underbelly, near his former space, berth 34a, and pictured as best I could the white car I'd seen in photographs but not yet in the flesh. After the other drivers had been herded upstairs I walked to the blue sedan now parked in its space, and crouched to look beneath its chassis. I don't know what I imagined I might find. There was nothing but the metal deck, stained with salt-encrusted rings of congealed fuel, but still I felt a fraction closer to my quarry.

Above deck I continued to shiver. Despite the grey cloudbank the sun's glare made me squint as I watched the shadow of land rise from the horizon ahead. Usually in such conditions I would wear sunglasses, but they remained in their case, as I wanted to replicate the view as Swift had seen it. Based on the meagre evidence of a few photographs and the testimony of travellers who claimed to have met him, he never wore eye protection.

'Maybe he wanted to see the world as it was, not filtered through coloured glass,' one American had offered.

Similarly, he had appeared to make do without a watch, mobile telephone, or indeed most of the items that modern travellers consider essential. A Marlborough Bay customs officer had confirmed as much.

'We stopped him. He looked freezing, with goosebumps and only wearing a t-shirt. Had only one bag. One pair of boots. His hair was all knotted, but we're used to seeing that. We gave him the questions and the pat down then looked in his car. Bloody mess, but nothing illegal.'

It's true what they say – we're all terror suspects now. Whatever your business, it won't stop guards from searching you and confiscating your contact lens fluid. Swift had come out clean, but this verdict hadn't prevented a newspaper from subsequently insinuating that drugs were somehow involved in his disappearance. After discovering a record of the customs check, all an astute local reporter had to do was ask unsuspecting members of the public what they thought the officers might have been looking for, 'Well, it could have been drugs ay, or, like, even a lighter. They're very strict these days.' Then, by publishing these quotes near to a helpful factbox on controlled substances, the editors planted seeds of suspicion in the public imagination, sensational new angles to catch the interest. It was classic tabloid architecture, as one of my tutors once referred to it, and it was working. People talked, 'Did you hear about the missing Brit? Yeah, they reckon he was into his dope, found pills in his car or something,' and newspapers were sold.

I lit up, leaning over to shelter the flame, and inhaled, watching the first curls of smoke whipping away on the wind and disappearing over the stern. The tobacco tasted earthy, stale and familiar, a reminder of the world I'd tried to leave behind.

As we approached the Marlborough Sounds, long green promontories reached out toward us like the splayed fingers of a great hand laid flat on the water. Surf curled around the tip of each headland, but as we motored into the channels between them, the surface calmed, until I could see the twin worlds reflected above and below the membrane.

As the boat slowed, its passengers came on deck to watch the passing land; lush green vegetation, sheer cliffs, jetties stretching out from rocks gently lapped by the sea. White birds with jagged wingtips circled the bays. Camera flashes lit the air as tourists tried to capture the view despite the poor evening light. Fiddling with buttons and dials, many looked down rather than out, their minds occupied with ambitions of showing friends back home how similar it all looked to the brochures.

A plump woman with a dishevelled beehive of brown hair was holding her daughter up to the rail, telling her about dolphins and whales. The girl stared, her arm outstretched but not pointing at anything in particular as her eyes chased the unfollowable movement of the surface where crests joined, split, dipped, rose and split again, reforming endlessly. She squealed as she was lowered back to the ground. Unsatisfied with her brief search for the creatures, she broke free and tried to pull herself up the bars, her tiny shoes slipping on the wet metal before her mother intervened.

I flicked my cigarette and watched it spin into the deep. The mist had turned to drizzle and my damp collar clung to my neck. Looking at the bush-strewn land I saw little sign of habitation, and wondered how it had appeared to early settlers. Men and women in canoes, their dark, tattooed faces burnt darker still by the exposure of long Pacific crossings. Then Dutch and English in wooden ships, powered by wind and oar, carrying flags, religion and gunpowder. Both parties would have seen what I now saw, little changed. A rugged land. Wild islands.

We neared port. It seemed ludicrously small considering the giant ships that docked there, and as we came alongside I saw that the ropes and cleats were giant too, dwarfing the men who heaved them into place. Far above them I could make out the caps of the high range that runs as a spine down the landmass, crossed only in a few places by roads and overgrown trails. I marvelled at its size, and as I leant to get a better look, shuddered at the thought that so much remained untamed. There was a lot of land out there for a man to get lost in.

Selected Poems

Nigel Pollitt

Tulips

The girl on the Tube has made the worst
roll-up I've ever seen. She holds it upright
like a vase. Threads of tobacco
like sphagnum moss peep from the top –
which is so wide you could plant tulips
in it. Years ago, before the ban,
she'd have lit up. Tulip smoke, matching
her pink woollen hat, would have coiled
to the stained ceiling of the carriage.

She looks like an elf, and has a stud
in her lip. She appears troubled and has
bright skin. Her jerkin is buttoned
tight. Her eyes flash that I'm staring.
Embarrassed, I offer tulips.
She smiles and takes off her hat. Amazement
shivers my face. *Don't say it*, she says:
Not a word. – But, I reply, *Your ears!*
– Would you like a cigarette? she asks.

She offers me tulips rolled in brown paper.
No one will notice – they're sleeping, she says.
You look like a —, I say, *and I think you
made them sleep*. Wearing her hat, my ears
grow pointy. The train breaks to the surface.
She rolls more tulips. Her mouth
is full of fire. The air is pink with smoke.
Outside, the night tells stories and fields
of tobacco flowers are listening.

Northern Line, Angel to King's Cross

Well before his jig is up
this dirt-jeans fiddler,
scallop eyes, cheek-to-cheek
moon smile, explains
(lips tight, not a word),
why for me they're just no fun
the others, the legal buskers. He's out

winging it, midnight prayer,
dirt nails skinning the fingerboard,
sparks like candles, like rain
and everyone in the hurtle
carriage – lots of nice, washed,
lovely-dressed people – is getting
ceilidh. Party girl goes *ooh*,

like a kid finds a fat stocking,
as if he's Santa – and we're all rapt
in this flash scurry of amped pentatonics
at the ridge of the plain world,
such twinkly light – and the *aah*
that sprays from his bow,
untoothed bow-saw, so tight strung

half the hoarse hairs snapped,
thousand years old, last few
calling the fizz, then off the fiddle
cap in hand reeling it in – look,
even the coppers, turning silver,
growing wings, flipping
into his hat.

New World

Hey –
I'm in America
With Americans in America
Everything here is in America
Nothing that's here is not in America

Air in America
Light in America
Nothing in me
is not in America

It looks like TV
It's not TV
It sounds like TV

Late-night bookstores
Homeless guys loading carts
Grackles pulling worms
Black squirrels in sumacs
eating walnuts
Hummingbirds
on the peppermint willow
More potholes than road

We're on the freeway
in the dark night
Bears asleep in dark America
Mountains dream in dark America

We're moving fast
Everything's zipping by
America's zipping by
Zip goes America
Zip it goes

Hey Nigel, says the tree
the old American tree

It's not a dream

say it

America America America

Candy and soda and guns and canyons

No one's been here before.

Slippage

The hand is in the dog's mouth
The hand is joking around in the dog's mouth

it makes a fist the dog likes
                                        to and fro they go

          dog bites soft dog knows how to bite
          press his teeth
               just right
          doesn't even think –

teeth slip press hard press tight hand pulls out
                                      Shoo! it says

It rings the phone rings
                    That's great says the man
              See you then

doesn't even think about it till – turns out – he's slipped
                                            a day
        a whole day

the date's a Tue not a Wed *Hell's teeth* and

he can't change his wife can't change   no one can alter

the arrangement that would have been
                                        so great
and now he can't touch the floor
          feel the door the dog
                              the old *Shoo!* dog

Up he slips the man slips in a tough bubble
through the kitchen
out the garden

    Mike!
    yells his wife
                  Daddy!
              scream his kids jump up
                            press fingers into

              the tough skin of the wrong day

can he even see hear them cry   Fetch a Ladder
                                    a Big Pin
                                    Down With Him!

in the swirly bubble ripping his diary   making snow

the dog watches the hand   make paper snow

Southwest Twizzle

Lauren Trimble

Excerpt from a novel

Beth Anne leaves with her Caramel Macchiato. There's nothing in the cup but de-puffed cream and half a caramel swirl, but she wants it as proof she's been somewhere. She's taken to visiting the local Starbucks in the late afternoon while Ronnie visits parishioners: the old, the infirm and (to her mind) the generally retarded. She likes the optimism caffeine gives her, but mainly she likes to listen to the students talk. The way their bright words jangle, how they arrange themselves in circles around their computers. Beth Anne carries a crumby black notebook in her purse and writes down words and bits of conversations. Today there's *gothic, oppression, fiscal* and *double fisting* on an otherwise blank page. The words are listed in capital letters. She runs an index finger over her pencil marks while she waits for the bus. Due to a semi-recent court ruling, she's not allowed to drive.

The bus, when it comes, is filled with sleepy evening commuters. Beth Anne takes a window seat. Being the end of November, the days are squished and the sun takes its leave around 6:30. The night-time reflections of the bus interior mix with the lights outside. The images run in opposing directions on the glass. Lit up buildings crash through faces and streetlights fly through trees. Beth Anne can see her face in alarming detail. Her once blonde hair faded to dishwater ash. Her cheekbones are obvious and sharp despite the plumpness in her arms and shoulders. It looks like a weight gain is ambushing her, overwhelming her and preparing an invasion on her cheeks. Wide-set, vaguely feline gray eyes give her face a heaviness that balances the displacement, a kind of gravity. She is striking, if slightly off-kilter.

She watches the empty, be-pot-holed lots of Target and Wal-Mart smear past the center of town. There's a tendency to build concrete fields for 10,000 customers where 200 (on a good day) might congregate. Her stop is a few miles off yet, in front of the local Albertsons, where the dinnertime rush has come and gone.

She scratches her knee and is newly shocked by the growth that spreads silky as loose panty hose down her calves and ankles, not as long or thick as she figured. She stopped shaving her legs when Ronnie grew his beard out.

'You look like a fucking hippie.'

He sniffed. He was liable to sniff when she swore. 'Jesus was a hippie.'

In the years since they moved to Utah, Ronnie wears long sleeves, despite the heat like an iron on his button downs. He likes his hair on the longish side: a protest against the clean-shaven, bicycling masses. His flock links him to Jesus and he's never quick to stop the comparison. He is, after all, Jesus' biggest fan. He makes T-shirts to this effect, which he sells to ironic Mormon teens from the back of his truck to burgeon the sickly offerings at his Baptist church, one of a handful outside Salt Lake City. Before she left for Starbucks today, Beth Anne voiced her misgivings.

'You think those Mormon mother fuckers won't bust you for selling illegally? This town is full of crew-cut-whistle-blowing-pieces-of-shit.'

When the bus drops her off, Beth Anne means to cross the parking lot and walk home, but she sees a shopping cart on the outskirts. It's knocked to one side and its position seems wrong to her. It is rusty and deranged, one of its wheels spinning creakily with a long *prinnn, prinnnn, prinnn*. She puts it right side up and it moves in a drunken, side swipe. The wheel that spun readily in the wind is sticky, marking her progress with random jerks. She walks it to the cart corral and notices another cart, further from the door. This one is crashed at an angle. On closer inspection its handle is warped, pushed to a V like someone knocked it over and jumped on it. This one barely stands. It takes nearly ten minutes to reunite it with the others. She finds six more. Some are covered in grease or missing wheels. There's physical relief to it. Things seem more whole when she's finished. This is how she used to feel about sex.

The lights are off in the house except for the runners in the kitchen. She has a hard time reading the note Ronnie put on the fridge:

I hope you got home safely. I know you're studying and that you'd rather not be disturbed. I also know you're a grown woman and that you don't like being checked up on, but can you tell me when you're going to stay late at the coffee shop?

There's macaroni in the fridge if you're hungry. I have to leave very early tomorrow morning to visit Mrs Johnson at the Logan hospital, so I've already gone to bed. I'll see you tomorrow.
   Yours in the love of Christ,
   Me

   She takes the paper down and puts it to her nose briefly before crumpling it to a tiny ball, flicking it to the floor. She hates the way Ronnie signs letters. Like Christ has forced his hand at feeling. She opens the fridge for the macaroni and finds a post-it note on the Tupperware with a smiley face. She eats the pasta cold, standing over the sink, and stares into the outside space hinted by the frosted window.

   On climbing into bed, Beth Anne is unable to suppress a feeling of expectation, of desire. She likes to imagine him in a crowd, going about his business, unaware of her. He looks tender, handsome, solid. Smiling at school kids and opening doors for the elderly. Everyone around is him gunmetal grey but he's in Technicolor, the real one there in the thick of it. He looks better, shinier in her head. She curls near him for warmth, facing him while he sleeps. Her fingers point to, reach for, but never quite touch his open mouth.

*

Beth Anne has begun to feel that life is a series of identical, empty boxes. Boxes she can see stretching all the way back to her childhood and (in the other direction) on to death. They aren't even nice boxes, but the cardboard kind you might buy at Ikea for storage. The difference between the past and future boxes is that the past ones might surprise with their contents, might be full of particular sunlight or powerful feelings. The new ones are empty without the prospect of fillings.

   She thinks about the past a lot now. The summer she met Ronnie in particular. She can no longer remember the moment she became aware of him. There were lots of strapping boys at camp. The Christian camp she and her sister attended frequently dangled sharp-chinned, blue-eyed specimens saying, 'Try not to look. NEVER touch.' The girls wore one-piece swimsuits, but the boys went shirtless. Beth Anne remembers lust as the way those boys clenched and unclenched their shoulders. How it felt to play 'chicken' in the lake, astride a male back, pushing other boys and girls into the water with the strength of her arms. The object was to knock your opponent off his or her steed, but for Beth Anne the real object was the moment someone fell and, grasping, pulled everyone down. She found it pleasurable to panic under water, surrounded by arms and legs and softer parts she couldn't always identify.

Her black, one-piece, camp-appropriate suit was a compromise. It was appealingly high on the bottom and low in the front, like a 1950s pin up. Her mother disapproved of its vague exposure of Beth Anne's recently acquired breasts, but she admitted that it was more 'decent' than the 'bikini number' Beth Anne tried on first. Thus began a series of advances and retreats on the topography of Beth Anne's body. The less she wore, the more her mother resisted and advanced, forcing Beth Anne to wear the shapeless cardigans and loose khakis she hated. 'No daughter of mine is going to be mistaken for a (she lowered her voice) street walker.' At camp, Beth Anne rolled the waistband of her shorts down and tied her t-shirts to expose her navel. Claire (the younger) pretended she didn't know her, which was fine by Beth Anne as Claire liked to quote bible verses at her in a pious, irritating voice.

Ronnie was the center of a group of particularly athletic boys. They did back flips off the dock and agreeably splashed the girls on the beach. Ronnie later told her it was her suit that caught his eye; so unlike the sporty ones most girls wore. From this Beth Anne gathered that he liked how her suit accented her cleavage. She liked the way his curly hair fell above his eyes and the way he held her glance like he was holding her face in his hands.

They were opposing sides in a game of chicken. He had a girl on his shoulders who was blonder and thinner than Beth Anne. Kirsty Swensen's inner thighs wrapped themselves around Ronnie's neck like a muscular, brown scarf. Ronnie squeezed the soft, ticklish part of her knee and she shook her tiny weight like a leaf falling graceful to his back. Kirsty Swensen was pious and nice and generously padded. She had memorized more Bible verses than anyone at camp and believed her first kiss would come from a pre-ordained husband. Beth Anne called her Kirsty Sucksen in her diary, taking care to make the K and S jagged and ugly, until they started to look like the letters Poison used on their album covers and Beth Anne had to start from scratch.

Beth Anne was astride the shoulders of Gabriel Dalston, who aspired to be a surfer but had only gotten so far as bleaching his hair. As the pairs charged, Beth Anne wanted a sheet, a burka, anything to hide from the eyes of Ronnie Stone as he turned his freckled face to the sun and looked right through the black spandex of her suit. He grabbed her foot when he was close. Beth Anne was sure it was nervousness that directed the kick she landed on Ronnie's face. The surprise jolted him and sent Kirsty flying. Kirsty toppled onto Beth Anne, who fell too, her arms swinging in wild circles, her legs choking Gabriel, who collapsed in a heap.

Dripping, Beth Anne rose from the shoreline sludge of Osprey Lake while the rest floundered. Ronnie was the second to stand, his nose dripping pink with blood and water. Beth Anne asked him how his face felt. 'How does it look?' he asked, 'because it *feels* like I got kicked in the teeth.'

In the seconds before Kirsty and Gabriel broke surface, Ronnie studied Beth Anne. Beth Anne squinted and studied Ronnie. She'd spent her tween years dreaming up the gauzy red of future loves (love always the important thing with sex going hand in glove, gauzier still in white, crisp sheets). 16-year-old Beth Anne would never have believed she would want this moment back, back when things were undone and the days weren't slick and uniform as raindrops on a windshield. Here was Ronnie, the first thing to ever happen to her, and she was already wishing for the next stage. If she could time travel for the purpose of smacking her teenage self, she would.

The Tulip

Rosie Miller

True to myself, I'd had a bit of a puff, and then I'd put on some shit film about this time traveller's girlfriend. She was just normal, couldn't travel through time like him. For some reason, I start to feel really broody after watching this crap. Well, not sure if *broody's* the right word to use here. But you know, I mean like *horny* – I use the word in that sense. But the problem when I've been on the puff is that my head's too buzzy and my limbs are too light to really sort myself out. So I just sit there on the sofa with my hand down my jeans, playing with my half-on until I fall asleep.

Don't know how long later, I wake to the sound of that familiar screaming coming from upstairs. Something I'm supposed to respond to. I stumble around the coffee table, bashing my shin, then drag myself up the stairs and push open the door to the baby's room.

– Daddy's here, Daddy's here… What's wrong now then?

Jackie's lying on his back in the pit of the cot, bawling his lungs out, little red fists shaking. I screw my knuckles into my eyes, which blocks everything out for a second, but when I look back into the cot, everything's sharper than it was before. So I fetch him up and start going up and down, wall to wall, my hand cupped around the back of his head. The greetings cards from when he was born are still tacked all over the walls. *Congratulations! It's a boy! What a joy!*

I press his arse-end against my face – all fine there – and he can't want *more* milk, can he? But he's showing no signs of settling, so I put him back down and go and make up a bottle for him in the kitchen. The screaming still feels like it's right inside my ears, but at the same time, miles away.

– I know, I know, Daddy's here…

I cluck at him as I go back in the room, *Daddy's here…*Then I kneel by the cot and reach in with the bottle. He won't take it. I try again, shoving the nipple into the dark, bawling hole. He starts to squirm up the mattress so I grab him by the leg and yank him back towards me.

– Oh come on, Jackie, for fuck's sake.

He screams louder and turns redder and kicks harder. He looks like he's about to split in two, and I can't take it no more. I let the bottle slip out of my hand; it rolls down the mattress and bangs into the panels at the end of the cot.

*

The next morning I'm back in *Morrison's*, buying even more shit. Sometimes I feel like I live here, I tell you. Little jars of mush. Wet wipes to clean up the mush. Another pack of those disposable bibs would be a good idea. It's expensive shit too – a pack of ten of these little cartons of special baby milk costs eight quid. Miss the days when he could just have the breast milk and be done with it. That stuff's *free*. Can't help smiling down at Jackie though, looking all cute, tucked up in his carry seat in the bottom of the trolley. Looks more like his mother every day. She died six months ago.

Turn down the aisle with all the toiletries and baby stuff and throw a pack of *Huggies* and a tub of E45 into the trolley. A few shelves along are the condoms – bright, shrink-wrapped boxes, all in a row. Pleasure, XtraPleasure, Ultrapleasure. I slow down, feeling like I might cry, right here, in the middle of bloody *Morrison's*. This is always the most difficult part of the supermarket.

Coz my fiancée was what you'd call a real go-er. If you know what I mean. She could *go*. I'm not ashamed of saying this: what I miss the most is the fucking. That's not me being shallow or anything – fucking was a big part of *who she was*, if that's the way you want to put it. Two, three times a night sometimes. As soon as I came through the door from work she'd be on me, trying to get at my shirt. Sometimes I'd even have to ask her to give me a bit of space, so I could to go to the toilet first, or have a sit down in front of the telly for a bit!

And she was into her toys, big time. We've got a glass one, a rubber one, and this sticky gel stuff that I used to rub on her that was supposed to make her tighter down there – *Geisha Gel* it's called. Got it online. And there's this really decent vibrator that I got for her last Valentine's Day. I mostly got it for a joke because it's called 'The Tulip' (that was my nickname for her, you see). She had a right laugh at that. Because if you think about it, a closed-up tulip flower does kind of look like a guy's helmet. I'd never realised that until I saw this. It's bright red and the end of it is shaped like a tulip.

But the thing is I don't know what the fuck to do with all the stuff in this drawer now. I haven't cleared it out, just left it as is. I mean, should I chuck them? Or should I use them on myself in some way? On someone else – if the opportunity presented? Sometimes I open the drawer and have a little smell or a feel. But I dunno, all these ideas are kind of weird maybe. The kinds of sentiments that make you feel a bit wrong in the head.

I also get scared that someone might go in that drawer one day. Like when her dad came over a few weeks after she died. He was taking away a few of her belongings, like clothes and jewellery. Her mum wanted them back. Anyway, at one point he went to open that drawer, and I had to say something. Like, um, I don't think you wanna bother going in there, John... Her dad's quite Christian; the whole family go to church on Sundays and all that. And he was obviously a bit distraught that afternoon. So it was important to stop the image of all that stuff in the drawer getting into his head. He don't wanna think of his daughter in that way. Especially when she's dead and he's trying to think of her in heaven with all the angels and what-not...

– Dan, mate! You alright? Looks like you're in your own little world there!

There was Terry, one of the lads from down the bus station where I work. Bit of a twat, to be honest.

– So how you both doing?

– Just trying to get on with it really.

– Yeah, you got to, for *his* sake, eh?

He reached down into my trolley and tickled Jackie on the cheek, a bit roughly actually.

– So when you coming back to us then? We got that Union strike end of the month remember...

– I dunno. Might not be worth it. Thought about coming back part-time, but turns out I'd actually have *less* money coming in if I do that, coz they'd slash my benefits.

– Well don't go mad will you, stuck looking after a baby all hours of the day! You get out much in the evenings?

– Nah. Not really. Might have a few people over to the house for a drink on my birthday next weekend. Seeing as it's my thirtieth and all...

—Ah, mate! You gotta do more than that for your big 3-O! How about we go into town? I know a couple good places we could go. *Qube?* That's new. You been there yet?

— No

— Ah, well we'll think of something — look — I gotta be off now. But give me a call alright?

— Sure. Take care, mate.

Driving buses. It's how I earn my living — well, used to... Nothing special, but I enjoyed it. Didn't have to think about anything when I was out driving. Sometimes I like to drive miles out of my way, just for the fun of it. Especially now — I just put Jackie in his seat with a bottle and it sends him right to sleep. Drove up the A1 the other day — got me all the way to fucking Scotland. Then just turned round and came back again. Yeah, I do miss the job. Well, I don't miss the passengers so much ('An empty bus is a happy bus!' is what we always used to say). But I do miss driving the buses.

I reach the checkout. The girl behind it starts clicking her tongue at Jackie and her eyes go a bit soft. She likes babies, but has obviously never had one before. Which I find quite sexy to be honest. A broody girl. Yeah, I'd give her one if I had the chance. Not that I know whether I should really be thinking about other women in that way yet. There's always the guilty head. But my unused body (and heart) is so fucking desperate.

Before getting back in the car when I come out of the supermarket, I sneak a bit of a happy puff in the car park.

— Let's go for a drive, Jackie...

I strap him into his seat in the front besides me, and then I just drive. Right out of Chelmsford, along the A12 for a bit, through the village where Tulip was born, then away into the proper countryside. I go round all these little bendy lanes for a bit, no idea where I'm going. Lots of them are blind corners, so I gotta go slow round these. All the colours of flowers blurring past on both sides in the spring. Pretty. Should drive out this way more often...The swaying and swerving soon sends Jack to sleep.

But as soon as he drops off, I suddenly get this Big Dread come down on me. I stop in a lay-by, an entrance to a field. The sun is pink and sinking. This is the kind of place where no one is, I think.

I turn off the engine and open the glove-box, quietly. I keep one of her thongs in here. I'm a bit sad when I realise that the smell on it is almost gone now. I reach down into my jeans. I'm ready and hard for once. My hand clicks with this arthritis-type pain. Fuck, my bones are done in with all this wanking already. I ignore it. But I've just started, when I see something coming towards me. It's a tall bloke with a stick. It must be the farmer who owns the land. Fuck, he's coming across the field, and he's staring right into the car at me the whole time. His little dog, some snappy terrier cunt, runs ahead and starts circling the car. I whip my hand out and sit up straight. The farmer is right in front of the car now. He lifts his stick, shaking a bit, and shouts through the glass at me.

— You oughta think about moving off my property! I'm gonna be bringing in some cattle through this gate shortly...

When I pull into the drive, Jackie wakes up and starts bawling. I take him inside, put him in the cot, and just shut myself in our bedroom across the way. Slumping against the door, I let out this sort of fucked-up high pitched laugh. Fuck, that stuff I smoked must've been strong. The mirror on the wall still has a heart with our names written in the dust. I go to the CD player and put on *Endless Love* (original Richie and Ross version). The screaming is almost drowned out. Then I crouch down and pull open the drawer in the bedside table.

I start to stroke the end of the Tulip one. I put my fingers to my nose. Dunno if it's her I smell, or just my imagination. Leaving the drawer open, I stand up and undo my jeans. Thing is, I really dunno what to think about when I'm doing this now though. I dunno if I should think of having sex with her, think about how soft and good her body was, to get off on the memories of us together. I mean sometimes that's the only thing that *can* finish me off – but sometimes she's the one thing I can't *stand* to think about. This time, I really want to think about her. Maybe I'm rubbing oil on her. Warm and slippery up against me. Rolling around. And, yeah, I think I'm getting close. But then the picture changes. Her bright eyes are closing as she leans over me. I try to get them open. Soon I'm scratching at them, and screaming at her to wake up. She collapses on my chest, her breathing all heavy and bubbly. She sounds like she did in those last few weeks with the pneumonia, the fucking pneumonia, so breathless that she wouldn't pick Jackie up and carry him around, scared as she was that she might drop him. I try to make her get up, but she's too heavy. So I just let her stay right there, and I stroke her hair and tell her I'll never leave her. 'Come,' she whispers, 'he comes, he does finally come...' I can't see through my watery eyes.

Porcelain Sunflower Seeds

Jenni Fagan

The bus smells of saliva, it's giving me the boak.
You were a seed twenty weeks ago, a one in four-hundred million ... chance at life. You beat the competition and now I'm half-vampire, my senses have never been so acute. I can still taste coffee from this morning, and I can smell lager a man behind me is drinking, and damp clothes. I can smell the dirt on the bus floor.

Down on the street, a newspaper man shouts and stamps his feet. The snow has not yet turned to slush but the streets are already a manky grey. I cannot wait to show you snow for the first time, let you feel the softness of snowflakes falling into your hand.

Trafalgar Square appears at the end of the road but the bus is stopped now, taxis are beeping and Nelson is scanning the horizon for what? Everywhere there are woolly hats, and umbrellas. This bus is going nowhere, and you are moving, and nobody knows you are here but me – they still only see one heartbeat, where really there are two.

The pavements are crammed. I tinker with my mobile, google, type in: How many people are there in the world?

There are six-billion, eight-hundred and eighty-four million, nine hundred and nine thousand, nine-hundred and fifty-three people on this planet. How do they count that? Does some wee guy go around the whole world toting up the score? As if. It's all done by statistics. That's all we are seed – statistics, numbers on a survey.

I read last week that people have started to have babies in secret, so they can supposedly be free. The secret babies don't have any numbers, no documents, no records. I won't do that with you. You can have a passport and be a statistic just like me. My name and numbers are in countless filing cabinets, it doesn't stop me being unique. It won't stop you either.

I keep my hand in my pocket, my thumb going over and over the sharp edges, the smoothness. We stole something this morning. I don't advocate theft of any kind, but this was an exceptional circumstance. I'll explain about those later.

First thing this morning, we had a coffee on the top floor of the

Tate Modern. I played you Nirvana Unplugged, then Song to the Siren by Tim Buckley. We went to see the Surrealists and I pointed out Picabia's The Fig Leaf. I told you about the Surrealists' first play, the one where the audience watched a bright blue curtain for two hours – then a fat woman, with gas filled balloons for breasts, came out and threw them into the crowd.

We browsed the Surrealist Manifestos and I explained that a rose, is a rose, is a rose. We are the penultimate expression of automatism. You. I. I know what you know, and I know that you hear me, everything, every heartbeat, every feeling that is mine is yours, and I am mindful of this all the time. When I curl up at night with your Dad – you know he is there, and you are happy. This is us.

One day I'll give you a wall in your bedroom to draw on, or maybe you will just chalk pavements like I used to. When we left the cafe on the top floor, I took a photograph of four silhouettes in a steel wall, four men staring at St Pauls, and I noticed that you, you were too still, too quiet – I tapped my fingers on my tummy. It wasn't until the Turbine Hall, that you began to move again.

There they were. Seeds. Hundreds of thousands of porcelain sunflower seeds covering the Turbine Hall. My heart was racing like it has been, since you began. My new bat-hearing tuned me into the crunch of porcelain under trainers, and I could almost see the fall of dust.

'Ma'am.'

The security man nodded, and I smiled. A Londoner with an unusual sense of decorum. I liked that. You kicked me, and I remembered the last exhibit we came to see. A huge cargo container lined with black velvet, and when we walked into it, it felt like disappearing – as the people around became spectre.

That's how I imagine death might be, a stepping off into the edge of darkness.

I'll tell you about death another day. It's nothing to fear. It'll happen to you, but hopefully it will happen to me a long time before you and I promise, if there is a cargo container on the other side of life, I will be there, for you, when you arrive, old and wizened, my little old man who once was a boy.

The air on this bus is damp. There is one old jakey sat up on the backseat. I touch the handful of seeds in my pocket, maybe there's twenty or thirty. I think you're sleeping. Sucking your thumb. Floating in space.

The jakey behind us cracks open another tin of lager, and he drops the one he has just crushed onto the floor. I glance back at him.

At least he's lost the shakes. I'll need to tell you about alcoholics one day, we have that gene but don't worry, the human soul is not currently understood by science. We have other genes as well, worse ones but if you have my will you'll be a natural non-conformist. It's a priceless attribute. Don't ever settle for thinking you have to be what they say you should be. I have not.

The porcelain seeds are smooth in my hand. I didn't know we were going to take them when we crouched in the gallery. I scooped some up and let them fall through my fingers just as a school boy wearing a Karate Kid t-shirt and a bandana lifted his foot up and stamped. Just like that. You kept turning around. I was thinking that the schoolboy wasn't even a seed when Karate Kid came out. His mate copied him and I flinched, turned a seed over in my finger. Each one was handmade in China, I pictured irate Chinese craftspeople marching in and slapping those boys about the head, all that work – to be stamped on!

These people cannot see you – seed. Bringer of bat-hearing, and visionary dreams.

I scooped up a handful and the security man looked at us.

'This is a rescue mission,' I told him.

He nodded. I closed my hand around the seeds and put them in my pocket. I smiled at the guy and he smiled back, and he thought there was two of us stood there, but really there was three. You settled down then, and we walked out, and down along the river. I'll take you there next year. There used to be wee beaches along it that people put deck chairs out on. They used to knit their own swimsuits once. Lots of things change. I'll tell you about Father Thames one day, but my version, I'll customise it just for you.

This bus is really not moving. The snow is falling again, and condensation runs in rivulets down the windows. One day I'll take you places where there's more trees than people, more snow than sky.

Nelson's hat has turned white, he stands watching over London like always. London. I don't know if you and me will stay here. It's not a place for seeds. Well, it can be but each day you walk among nine-million people, and you know what it is to be unseen.

I don't want you to feel unseen, or muted, or like you are an uninvited stranger in an unexplainable place. Not ever. I want to raise you by the ocean so you'll know why we're here but if I can't get us out, and we have to stay here in a flat, I will still find a way to show you the skies.

The truth of it is this seed – we live in a world without explanation, in a galaxy and universe surrounded by galaxies and universes and nobody asks questions too loudly because the answers are sketchy at best.

The earth is an island, floating in space. It is a pinprick on a pinprick. And we are, all of us, crazy islanders and I will not ever be able to explain to you – why we arrive as seeds, and leave as dust.

But, I can show you the truth in rainbows. I can bake you caterpillar chocolate-cakes and take you out to the park in autumn so we can kick up the leaves.

Here we are.

Two heartbeats.

You. And me.

Just sitting on a bus. The taxis are honking furiously again and the sign at the front of the bus is changing from Tottenham Court Road to This Bus Terminates Here. I pick up my scarf and the bus driver's speaker crackles away and I do not know how long we have sat here. The jakey's gone.

Pull my hat down hard, tie my scarf and hold the handrail as we go down the steps. I'm wearing wellies, and jeans, and my jacket is zipped up to my chin. I'd never wear wellies before but you make me want to keep my feet dry.

We step onto the pavement and an old man swerves by us, he is singing a song loudly in Italian. His coat is covered in shiny badges. He gestures at the people, as if he is ushering them off a plane and they try and avoid him, he catches my eye and I half-smile.

This is the world seed. In all its smelly glory. I hope you can forgive me for bringing you into it, especially if you think too much like I do.

But it's okay really, the ache, the living, the beat of your own heart. The silence of unanswerable questions. There are shooting stars and music – there is magic if you learn how to look, and it is still our world, no matter how many other people might try and convince you, it's mostly theirs.

It is yours and it is mine.

And all these other people walking by us in the snow, it's theirs too. I touch you, and I know you are awake again, and the sunflower seeds in my pocket are smooth under my fingers. We can wait a few years, then we will go and plant them – somewhere where there is a view. We'll let them nestle in the cool soil and water them on weekends. After all, who says – that porcelain seeds can't grow?

Selected Poems

Marion Ashton

The Hide

Last light on the last day
of the year, the low realms of sky
an unlikely sequence of horizontal stripes -

indigo, turquoise, magenta – down
to where the sinking sun spreads
red ink across the furthest reed-pool.

Midnight will be difficult. Five of us,
not six, this year. What to say.
Still unthinkable that he could leave.

Within the hide's ritual hush
lenses point and move in unison,
slaves to the marsh-harrier's every breath-

held glide, dip, rise, loop and dive.
I watch you, friend of forty years,
lost in the bird, your features slackened,

unguarded. On the marsh, the hawk flickers
to ground, and if he rises one more time
it will be too dark for us to see.

Modigliani and Spiders' Webs

                8.40am 13th October 2010,
the Modigliani post-card slipped
from the notebook's pages: 'Seated Nude,
1916' – the one you stood before for minutes
at the Courtauld, trying to fix the very red
of that drape – claret red of blood and desire,
the wall's smudged pale teal, the terracotta
flush of the eyes-closed face, peach-yellow
the long body, black commas of pubic hair,
that elliptical dark brushstroke tracing the swell
of ochre thighs.
                Autumn sun on the kitchen
window lights up the spiders' webs, silvering
each spoke, each concentric link and thread
of their fine-denier construction: ethereal,
aerial bridges, suspended wall to sill, flexing
with each breath of wind, precision engineered
for sensation, entrapment, and tensile strength.
On the television screen, Osman Araya, the sixth
San José miner, emerges from the rescue capsule
into the light, hugs his wife like never before.

33 Chilean miners, trapped underground for 69 days, were brought to the surface one by one, in a rescue capsule, on 13th October 2010.

The Viewing

Strange to have got to fifty, and never seen
a dead person, not even an open coffin.
Anthea has seen dozens; talks of joking
with other nurses behind the laying-out screen.
The closest I ever came was a film viewing
at the Tate Modern: by flickering light
in a dark booth, I watched the artist's mother die,
twice over, heard her last-breathed, catching
sigh. When Dad died, it came out of the blue:
keeled over on Blackpool beach, feeling dizzy.
It was two days before someone said *aneurism* –
too late by then. Mum and Anthea went to view
the body, to save us the trauma. I complied.
He should have been the first; I never said goodbye.

Before the Demolition

It was that bonfire by the river – the one
she lit when no-one was around
the one that makes her eyes water
each time she remembers the smoke,
the flames, the embers, the ashes –
where she burned the black piano her mother
had taught her to play – no room for it
in the new house – along with the oak dresser,
the chair her father died in, tilting mirrors
which flickered with the faces of ancestors,
the gramophone, the college trunk:
all stuff which had a place in the old house,
regardless of uneven walls, flagstone
floors, thatched eaves full of nesting birds.

Deeping Locks

Squeeze through the kissing-gate,
        stuck fast in long grass –
only the lithe can get in –
        climb down the bank: wet hedges,

dog-rose, nettle, civet scent of wild garlic,
        rampant bindweed tangle –
round the bend to the cascade's din.
        Catch the pheromone of eel and stickleback.

See where the Welland picks up pace, drops
        headlong over the ledge in a crash of foam.
Watch the boys balance high on the edge
        of the lock-gate, jack-knife and dive, down

into dark waters, slippery as otters.
        Wade out from the shallows – felt of wet fern
between the toes, sparks of minnows
        across white thighs. Slide under.

At Abu Dhabi Airport

He watches her progress
  down the long escalator
    to the marbled Departure Lounge.

He can tell it's a young body
  beneath the head-to-toe black
    of burqa-jilbab and veil:

it's in the upright bearing,
  the backward toss of the head,
    the clear brown eyes, scanning

the hall with unveiled disdain:
  unsettling how they're framed
    in that narrow, peep-show slit.

A gust of cool air blows
  the long cloak apart,
    revealing a shock of yellow

leather mini-skirt, stretched tight
  across smooth, bare thighs.
    She appraises him, unblinking:

American businessman – oil,
  most likely: forties, crisp blue shirt,
    sharp-creased Chinos, cell-phone,

laptop, gold watch, wedding ring
  red-faced. They both know
    this image will stay with him forever.

Evensong

We're watching colour drain
from high windows, dissolve
on stone flags – fidgeting
in the choir stalls through a litany
of readings, psalms, sermons, prayers –

> secret breasts beneath
> my blue robes, Friday's Youth Club,
> Alex Walker, kissing with tongues – waiting

for the recessional hymn:
the slow file in pairs back
between the rows of pews, past
the warbling voice, past our parents,
past the black-feathered hat, the swaying man –
to gather round the vicar
near the bell-tower, for the Benedict –

> *The grace of our Lord Jesus*
> *and the love of God,*
> *and the fellowship of the Holy Ghost*

soft shufflings from the congregation,
gathering gloves and prayer-books;

> *be with us all ever more – Amen..*

At last we throw off the robes,
sling hats on pegs in the damp-book vestry; burst
out of the porch door into the kingdom of freedom,

> *the power and the glory for ever and ever*

run headlong home in the dark.

Abundance

Carl Newbrook

From the opening of a short story

The moment I put my head down I knew I wasn't going to sleep. Two pillows and I'm propped like a dowager, one and I'm pinned to the mattress. The duvet's heavy as a horse blanket. I should lever myself out of bed to open the sash, but then we'd get the grunt and grind of the traffic. Over-ate this evening. I knew it, I couldn't stop myself. Heartburn, I deserve heartburn. If only I could lie on my side. My babies have settled though, somehow they must know it's night-time. Seven weeks and four days to go. *Three* days; we're well past midnight. How could I have forgotten this part, the waiting to get back to normality?

Charlie's dead to the world, thank God. I couldn't talk to him. The kitchen is blitzed and he says, 'Marianella will be here in the morning'. His definition of nannying isn't mine. She's not 'staff'. Creased into the pillow, his face, before I put the light out. With his hair over his eye he looked boyish, the lanky boy on our first date. Now when he throws his arm over me in the night it's all I can do to lift it off me. Exercising bores him, then again he doesn't have the time. He can get a full eight hours tonight, I can't begrudge him that. He only sees Olivia at the weekend.

Being awake at least means I'm avoiding my new, all-is-lost dreams. Arriving home to find the house has been stripped, to floorboards and bare plaster. Or the key doesn't work and I can't get inside. Or the house has gone, swept away in a flood. Nightmares where I come to, gasping for breath, as if some malignant thing is squatting on my chest, squeezing the life out of me.

At best I'll doze, surfacing at each snuffle on Olivia's monitor. And at first light, sixish, I'll be awake for good. And then Olivia will be awake and wanting to be fed and entertained. Seven weeks and three days.

I don't know why I thought of Margaret tonight. Half-listening to the chatter at the dinner table, I did the calculation and realised it was fifteen years ago. I was a different person, everything was different. I was sure I hadn't thought of her since that day, not once. Margaret.

We called her Maggie, didn't we? I don't remember her surname. There must have been a trigger to bring her back to me, a word, a phrase. I don't like the idea that our minds, our lives are random. A programmer ought to believe in order. Code is more reliable than the human brain. It doesn't forget and it can move mountains. Margaret... Margaret... No, the name's gone.

We were out back, I remember that, the two of us, next to Goods-In, sitting on those hard plastic chairs. Smokers' Corner, a concrete yard with a pile of butts under the ledge, where we had our morning and afternoon cuppas, fifteen minutes to ourselves. It was my last day. Goodbye drinks with the women at the shop, then a blow-out in town with friends, a crawl, the Bigg Market, finishing at a club. Margaret was sucking her way through a cigarette. Her face was blanched and her hands were trembling. When she spoke, she didn't look at me. 'Can I tell you something?'

I looked around the table and tried to replay the last few conversations in my head. Rachel had been telling us, hands flapping, about a business jolly to Paris, on Eurostar. The unexpected swankiness of St Pancras and the snootiness of the guards replying in idiomatic English to her decent French. How a silver-haired Gallic sugar daddy in a cashmere coat and silk scarf had flirted with her, in his accented English, which she took off to a T. She claimed he owned some vineyards in the Camargue and that he'd offered her, without ever saying the words, a night at the Crillon. A classic Rachel story, putting herself at the centre of an unlooked-for drama, emerging safe and sound, with lots of jokes and slapstick along the way. Hard to know when she's crossed over into make-believe. I don't think she knows either.

'You minx! You didn't tell *me* all this!' Nick exclaimed, staring at her, then glancing at each of us in turn, playing the outraged husband.

What did she say? 'Darling,' – you knew a line was coming – 'he was barely a *euro* millionaire.' Her cocked wrist adding a nicely judged flourish to the gag. I don't know anyone who enjoys their life as much as Rachel. She hasn't changed, she was just the same at college when she didn't have two pennies to rub together.

Nick, the one true Londoner, the rest of us are incomers, had talked about the new station and the changes around King's Cross. The destruction of the Stanley Building and the daft notion of constructing a set of apartments inside a gasometer. That the prostitutes – 'working girls' he called them – had been dispersed and the trade pushed northwards, up York Way. A proportion of the women were trafficked and the rest on drugs; some pimped, some independent. The irony that the influx of construction workers had created a demand for paid sex. Nick will forget he's not conducting a meeting at his production company. London is *his* London. A high-horse kind of guest when he's drunk.

Before Nick built up a head of steam, I passed another bottle of Pinot Noir round the table and we each pitched in with our own St Pancras tales.

Tori had bought a pair of silver earrings in a shop called Fossil. Charlie liked the champagne bar for an occasional Friday night snifter on the way home. I had to act amazed: the last-to-know wife. Nick explained how the original station was built with an understorey to hold barrels of beer, brought down every day from the Midlands, how the dimensions of the space were dictated by the size of the giant barrels. Rachel slapped the table and declared the lovers' statue, the Backpack Bombers, the ugliest in London. I bit back a smile because I could tell by the spasm of confusion on Tori's face that she liked the statue and couldn't understand why anyone would object to it. As ever, she and Rachel were at cross purposes. Someone said how difficult it was to create life-like sculptural trousers. Someone else mentioned hair and spectacles.

I talked about walking along the canal, back in the spring. I was out with Olivia in her pushchair. By the Maiden Lane Bridge, on the other side of the canal, a pair of swans had constructed a nest, a six-foot span. It was made with dead vegetation and rubbish, rotting polythene, plastic bags, lengths of fluorescent twine, a recycling project. Like a lot of my stories it didn't have an ending. I wish I had a portion of Rachel's confidence and could speak fluently and amuse people the way she does.

None of this seemed to have any connection with Maggie, or the me, back in Newcastle, that was seventeen years old.

Then Myles started up. While he talked, I remembered how one of the swans that day had waddled into the water with a splash. Olivia was asleep. If I'd shown her the swan she'd have frowned and pointed, 'No!' The white of the bird made the murk of the water look even filthier. A Smirnoff bottle floated by and the glass twinkled. Walking back, the sun was hot on my face, I had to use my free hand to shield my eyes against the glinting light. By the lock, heat pulsed off the flaking brick wall, and up ahead I could see the miraged air quivering. In the scrubby verge, flowers were coming up. I stopped to run a silver-haired catkin through my fingers. Spring was hurtling forwards. The sun, the water, the greens, it was a rare moment of bliss. A feeling took hold of me, impossible to describe. I felt heavy, moored, and at the same time light-headed, light-bodied. I translated the feeling, an at-home feeling, into a word I could understand – abundance. I thought how happy I was and my eyes filled with tears because the moment was already fading.

Myles got his elbows spread on the table, with his bulldog head lowered, which meant he was in for the long haul. What is it in men – some men – that they *know* they've got the right?

I kept going back to Maggie and Newcastle. Maybe it was something I'd overheard Ella and Rick say? They were at the other end of the table, whispering to each other, heads bowed, almost touching, half-hidden behind the candelabra. I'd tried to keep them apart, Ella ignoring me when I ushered her towards a chair in the middle of the table. She actually pretended not to hear me, like a child. My little sister, the black sheep; she knows she can get away with being churlish. Over the years she's had a lot of practice. How they look at each other, Ella and Rick, the hunger. I thought they'd have outgrown that stage. They met – what? – eighteen months ago now, at a demonstration, a fact that Ella wears like a medal. Rick's serious, not much to look at. Ella's changed, forever banging a drum for some cause or other. The news is terrifying enough without her playing the north London Cassandra. I was grateful for their whispering. If Ella had joined the general conversation she'd only have hectored us about our collective failings. For her, 'middle class' has become a term of abuse. We get on by ourselves, but she can't spare an evening apart from Rick. When she was a girl I mothered her; lately, I've found I'm willing myself to be happy for her.

Myles rumbled on about the family's summer holiday in the Swedish lakes – *a land of milk and honey, three hours from civilisation, pricey but worth every penny*. Tori, the trouser-wearer in their marriage, added clarifications, her nostrils flaring each time. Her interior design business goes, she tells us, from strength to strength. A power-dressed cheerleader for herself, her non-stop American vim leaves me feeling wan and washed-out. English reticence and self-effacement doesn't charm her, it baffles her. I see her looking around, inspecting; she's itching to give our home a personalised makeover. Their Dulwich house is a World of Interiors showcase. I admire her and would hate to be one of her clients.

With Myles a story has to be told, *hm*, from the beginning; to the, *ah*, middle; to the, *um*, end. He dots Is and crosses Ts and isn't embarrassed to say so either. He uses clichés with such gusto he tricks you into thinking he's saying something original. I suppose his thoroughness is what makes him a good banker. Though, in fact, I don't know what a banker does, good or bad. I've never been able to take in much of what Charlie's told me. Acronyms, jargon, consultant-speak, barrow boy chipperness. Possibly I don't ask the right questions. Yes, that could be it. I can't get beyond the notion that the whole shebang is a form of disorganised gambling, with other people's money. Confidence is key, I know that much. Charlie seems to be a winning gambler. He's still at his old firm, the credit crunch didn't affect him. His chips continue to accumulate. Anyway, he doesn't like to talk about his day at the office. Charles, in my limited experience, is a typical man: compartmentalised. He would rather hear about whatever Olivia's been up to. And he wouldn't want to hear about tears by the canal, or memories of Maggie and Newcastle.

No Long Way Round

Saskia Sarginson

Chapter One

We weren't always twins. We used to be just one person. The story of our conception was the ordinary kind they tell you about in biology lessons. You know how it goes: an athletic sperm hits the egg target and new life forms.

So there we were, a single ho-hum baby in the making. Then comes the extraordinary part, because that one egg split, tearing apart like a ripped blanket, and we became *two* babies. Two halves of a whole. That's why it's weird but true – we were one person first, even if only for a millisecond.

Issy and I used to wonder which of us was the original singleton, the poor saddo halfling. And which of us peeled apart, like a shadow slipping free, sliding away, unattached but irrevocably linked. The other question that made us talk in hushed whispers was 'suppose the separation had come too late?' because of course then we would have been Siamese twins, destined to be stuck fast to each other like the people in the fairy tale about the magic turnip, forever welded on.

We'd seen a picture in 'The Book of the Weird and Wonderful' of Siamese twins. Except that 'Siamese' isn't the right word. Apparently it's better to say 'conjoined'. The blurry photograph was confusing. It took us a while to work out what we were looking at, because at first we couldn't believe that it could be real – two creatures, two *girls,* sharing one head. But this was what the photograph showed us (it's the honest-to-goodness truth). Picture it in grainy black and white: two pale creatures with four entangled arms, three legs and one head between them. The head was looking right at the camera with sad eyes and a twisted mouth, as if she was grimacing at some invisible pain. We read the blurb underneath. The girls had been abandoned at birth and kept locked away in a Russian institution for their whole lives. I had nightmares afterwards, waking in the dark, grabbing at phantom limbs pushing through my sweating skin. I'd rolled closer to Issy in our double bed, needing her smell and the rhythm of her sleeping, nudging into her dreams.

Even now I read stories about twins if I can find them. There's not much else to do in here except read. Read and daydream. Myths are full of twins. Castor and Pollux, Apollo and Artemis. Romulus and Remus. That was our favourite story. It wasn't much of a leap for Issy and me to imagine having a wolf for a mother. We liked the idea. We played the 'suppose' game – suppose we'd lived in the forest when we were little? Suppose our mother had been a wolf? Then we would have gone creeping behind her as she prowled the undergrowth, wild-eyed and fierce, waiting to spring out on the men from the Forestry Commission with open jaws, tearing the heads off campers and caravaners.

There's a Greek myth that says if a woman sleeps with a god and a mortal on the same day she'll have two babies: one child from each father. Even our mother wouldn't do anything as slutty as that. But when we climbed the branches of the lilac tree to sit on the roof of the shed, sharing an apple and discussing possible paternal options, the idea of being fathered by a god was satisfying. The obvious choice was a rock god. Our mother played The Doors obsessively. She looked at Jim Morrison's picture on the album cover and sighed. The only thing that we knew about our father was that our mother met him at a commune in California. Bingo. It had to be Morrison. We didn't want our dad to be one of the creeps and weirdos we lived with in Wales. Lanky Luke or smelly Eric. Mummy didn't love any of them. We wrote Mr Morrison a letter once, secretly. We never got a reply. We probably got the address wrong.

On the 3rd July 1971 Jim Morrison was found dead in his bath in Paris. Cause of death: heart failure brought on by heavy drinking. He'd planned to stop being a rock god and become a poet. He'd been waiting for his contract to run out. The day the news broke we came home to find our mother sobbing; she played Hello I Love You over and over, and wept into her glass of red wine. We cried too. We threw ourselves on our beds and howled. At first it was a kind of show; but then fake turned to real. You know how sometimes when you laugh really hard you can trip some emotional switch and start crying instead? This was a bit like that. Except pretend crying tripped the real thing - a great tidal wave broke through us and we were drowning in tears, taking shuddering gasps of air, snot smearing our cheeks, our heads nearly bursting. We frightened ourselves so much we ran downstairs so that we could cry in the same room as our mother; her sobs got louder as we opened the door. Later, when she was sober and we were all hiccupping and squinting through our swollen eyes, Mummy told us that Jim Morrison definitely, without-any-doubt, wasn't our dad. 'Ridiculous,' she said wistfully, 'where on earth did you get that crazy idea?'

We tried a few more times to discover who our father was. But Mummy got irritated. Shrugging and rolling a cigarette slowly, she'd blow smoke spirals and look disappointed by our dull questions. 'I've started a new dynasty,' she explained once. 'I want you to build your own future. You don't need a past.' We knew that she thought our desire for a father was petty and bourgeois. All the worst things in the world were petty and bourgeois. We stopped asking.

The country was going to hell, Mummy said, what with the miner's strike and all those three-day weeks. Ted Heath was a bloated fool. We had to be prepared for the worst. We needed to be self-sufficient. She dug up the weedy flowers and planted vegetables and brought two nanny goats: Tess and Bathsheba. One brown and the other black, they both had switchy tails and cloven feet like the devil. We wanted to love them, but they just chewed all day, grinding their long teeth, looking past us with marble eyes, ignoring us even when we squatted to scratch their ears. The goats broke free of their tethers every day and trampled the vegetable patch, pulling up plants by the roots. Every morning, Mummy spent grim hours trying to replant the severed broccoli and carrots before she sat with her head buried in a fidgeting goat's flank, fingers working, swearing, to emerge with thin milk rancid as old cheese or stewed socks.

She had a book showing which wild foods were safe to eat and when and how to pick them and cook them. That book was read like the Bible in a house of preachers, consulted constantly, pondered over, worn and stained from being taken along on walks and splattered from being propped next to the stove. Foraging became a new religion. Plucking berries and mushrooms and apples from the hedgerows – now, Mummy said, that was free-spirited *and* free. Two things she did approve of.

We got scratched from pushing through brambles to get at the crab apples, our mother directing us from the path, barefoot, tossing her hair impatiently; 'Higher girls. That's it. Get the ones on the next branch up.' She made jelly and wine from those: tangy tasting and pink as a tongue. Once we got terrible stomach cramps from some speckled mushrooms she'd put in a stew. But we got to like brain fungus fried in butter with salt and pepper and a little curry powder; a crinkly, rubbery, pale green fungus that grew at the foot of pine trees – we tore up handfuls whenever we found it. And puff balls, picked when they were fat and white, rolling in the dewy grass on autumn mornings like misplaced snowballs. We had them sliced in batter for breakfast with crispy bacon.

*

Have you ever felt real hunger pangs? Not just a growl, the casual complaining of your stomach missing a meal, the inconvenient rumble and gurgle when lunch is late. I mean the deep birthing pain of true emptiness. The hollow ache of nothing.

Think about it. Birds are light as a handful of leaves. They don't stuff themselves with huge plates of greasy food. People will get angry with you. They'll say: for heaven's sake, you hardly touched your lunch! You've got an appetite like a bird! And that's good. The less you eat the more your stomach shrinks – withering up like a flat balloon. Of course, it hurts. But you can use those pangs like a knife to slice out all the bad things inside you. Eventually you'll come to crave that feeling. Because hunger is a friend. With it you can get down to your bones quicker than you'd think. I feel them under my fingers, nudging up close below my skin, closer every day: smooth and flawless and hard. That's what everyone says about bones, don't they? That they're pure. Clean. I trace the lines of mine and they make a shape: the scaffold of myself.

It's all we are in the end anyway. Sometimes not even that. Sometimes there aren't even bones to show for a life – just molecules shifting in the air – and maybe a few memories locked up in your head that have got yellowed as old photographs.

I'm tired now. I'd like to go back to sleep. I'm rambling. I know I am. Issy wouldn't like it. She told me to shut up when we had to sit in that little room with those two women asking us the same questions over and over.

What did we do? What did we see? What time, and when, and where?

'Don't say anything, Vi,' Issy said. 'You don't have to say anything. They can't make you.'

And she holds my hand tight, her curled fingers squeezing hard, steely as a trap.

Ava Gates

Kristina Heaney

An excerpt from the novel

Entering the restaurant Mike was hit by a chorus of Mambo Italiano, cranked up on the sound system to compete with the heaving lunchtime service. He spotted his mother first, wedged into one of a line of booths in the centre of the room. The tabletop was acting as a shelf for her bosom. Jack's figure, tiny in comparison, was crammed in next to her. He had crayons and appeared to be doodling across the paper tablecloth. His father sat opposite them. He had put down the newspaper for once and replaced it with the menu. Mike's stomach groaned; he'd lost his appetite. He could turn round right now and leave. Get in a taxi and head for the station.

'Darling? Darling? Darling we're over here.' She was waving one of her big arms above her head to assist him. 'Over here sweetie.' Just like being fifteen again.

He began squeezing through the packed restaurant to where they sat. A spasm of giddiness pulsed through the muscles in his legs with each step, settling in his gut. He'd felt something similar for weeks before Jack was born; 'The Weight of Responsibility' his father had called it. A waiter was giving a half-arsed rendition of Happy Birthday as he placed a cake in front of a little girl, her ice cream grin wide.

Mike reached the booth and hesitated, unsure of whether to announce himself in some way or just plonk into the space next to his father. After several silent seconds his mother made the decision for him.

'Well, what are you standing there for? Sit down and say hello to Jack.'

'Right, yeah,' he mumbled, dropping into his seat. His father glanced up at him, raising his eyebrows before returning to the menu.

'Aren't you going to take your coat off?' his mother said.

'Yeah, that makes sense.' He stood up again, untangling himself from his jacket sleeves. He glanced around for a hook or a hat stand but there didn't seem to be one.

'Oh, give it to me. I'll put it with mine and Jack's.' She took the coat out of his hands and folded it into a neat bundle. It disappeared under the table and into one of her shopping bags.

Mike slid into his seat again and stared at the crown of the boy's head. His face was low to the table as he meticulously coloured a green triangle. It was clear from the look on his mother's face that he was meant to say something now.

'Hey Jack, how's it going?' Mike ventured.

'Stop colouring in and answer your father properly Jack.'

Mike bit his lip. It would be so much easier just to let him carry on colouring. The boy laid his crayon down, lining it up against the saltcellar so it wouldn't roll away. 'Hi Dad,' he said, his face solemn as he met Mike's gaze.

Mike attempted a sincere smile but he was struck again, as he always was, by the child's growing resemblance to him: the same flat brown eyes, the straight, tapering nose, the same widow's peak, though Mike's could only be seen in old photos these days. He didn't appear to have inherited anything from Lisa at all. Even the boy's hands, now tracing the outlines of his pictures on the tablecloth, were smaller copies of his own. Wasn't it bad enough that he was far bigger than the last time Mike saw him? Did the child have to be the spitting image of him as well? The Weight of Responsibility pitched in his stomach.

'How's school?'

'Alright.'

'Just alright? Not good?'

'It's alright.'

'You playing lots of football?'

'No. Why would I be playing football? Football's rubbish.' Jack wiped his nose on the sleeve of his sweatshirt and picked up a yellow crayon.

'Don't do that, it's disgusting,' Mike's mother said, thrusting her napkin into the boy's face. He batted it away and went back to his drawings.

'Everything on this menu is beige,' Mike's father said, tossing the laminated cardboard down onto the table. 'Beige pasta in beige sauce. Beige chips. Beige potatoes.' He took up the menu again.

'Pork escalope,' he read. 'Beige. Garlic bread. Beige. Pizza with a white sauce; no tomato. Beige. Look at that food under the hot lamps.' He pointed towards the open range kitchen. 'Not one of those plates has got anything green on it. These chain restaurants are all the same. Clearly an *Italian-American Dining Extravaganza*,' he reeled from the menu's masthead, 'is code for deep fried and overpriced.'

'Oh Leonard. Why don't you have the soup?'

'What flavour is it?'

Mike grinned. 'Beige I imagine.'

His father stared at him. Mike's smile dropped as the old man sighed and turned away.

'Can I get you any drinks at all to start with?' A girl in a stained red apron hovered at the edge of the table. Mike craned his neck round to see the names on the beer taps at the bar.

'Just a jug of water for the table, that's all,' his mother said.

'Great.' The waitress swirled a biro across her pad and marched off to see to other diners.

'Great,' Mike repeated. His mouth had gone dry. 'Doesn't he want a coke or something?' He asked, nodding at Jack.

'We discussed it in the car and I said he could either have a glass of coke with his lunch or an ice cream afterwards but not both and he's chosen the ice cream. Isn't that right Jack?'

'Mmm,' the boy said, picking up the blue crayon. 'Can I have pizza?'

'Yes, you can have pizza. But remember, you've got to finish it.' She picked up her napkin and licked it. Mike fought the childhood reflex to cover his own face with his hands as she dabbed it against a speck of something on Jack's cheek.

'Grandma, stop it. I'm fine.' He elbowed her off him and she relented.

'What are you having darling?'

'It's fine Mum, I'm not hungry.'

'Don't be silly, you've got to have something to eat. You can't sit here with nothing in front of you while we're all eating.'

'Fine.' He glanced down at his menu and chose the first thing his eyes fell on. 'Steak sandwich. That'll do.'

The waitress reappeared with the water and four empty tumblers.

'What's the soup?' Mike's father asked.

'I think it's butternut squash.'

'Beige,' he grunted. 'Fine, I'll have a bowl of that. No bread roll.'

'And then we want one Margarita pizza, the Mediterranean chicken with a jacket potato and the steak sandwich and chips. Okay?' his mother said, looking up at the waitress.

'Great.' She finished scribbling and was gone.

'What are you drawing there mate?' Mike asked, squinting at what looked like a lopsided hourglass encased in a thick black circle. 'Is it a...' He couldn't even hazard a guess; drunken road sign was the best he could come up with.

'It's an Omnitrix,' Jack said, keeping his head to his work. 'It's not all the right colours 'coz these are all the crayons they've got but that's how it looks.'

'And what's an Omnitrix?'

'You know, from Ben 10.'

Mike looked at his mother and mouthed, 'What's Ben 10?'

'It's a cartoon. Jack loves Ben 10, don't you darling.'

'It's sort of like a watch but not 'coz you can like transform into different stuff like aliens with it.'

'Wow. That's quite a watch mate.'

'Yeah, everyone has them at school.'

'What, toy ones?'

'Durr Dad, 'course they're toy ones. It's not real, it's just a cartoon.' The boy looked up at him, his head cocked to one side, as though he were sizing him up, checking for weaknesses.

'Well, do you want one?' Mike asked. 'A Ben 10 watch thing?'

'An *Om-ni-trix*.'

'Alright, an Omnitrix, smartie-pants. You know, for your birthday present.' He'd wanted to arrive with a gift for the missed birthday but he'd been too busy with other things to think about what to get him. Fucking Ava, she was taking over all his headspace; he didn't have room to think about anything else. If it weren't for her he'd be okay at stuff like this. He wouldn't fuck it up. 'We could go and get it this afternoon. Straight after lunch if you want.'

'Nah.'

'Nah?'

'I've already got one. Mum's friend Kieran got it for me.'

'Oh right. And who's Mum's friend Kieran?' Mike tried to watch his mother's face for a reaction – she handled everything when it came to Lisa – but she had suddenly become very interested in the texture of the tablecloth.

'Oh, you know, just her friend. They go to the cinema and to restaurants and stuff like that.' He added a thick green outline to his picture. 'Sometimes they take me with them and sometimes not and Natasha from up the road comes and babysits me. But I'm not a baby. I don't mind 'coz she plays games with me.'

'And where do you all go when you go with them?'

'The park sometimes. One time we went bowling and they have these special things that pop up so the bowling ball doesn't go down the sides and you always knock some of the skittles over. That way you can always win.'

'Does your mum have a lot of friends that are like Kieran? Friends that are boys?'

'Michael,' his mother said, a pleading look creasing her forehead. She knew he hated it when she called him that. Only one person had ever been allowed to call him that.

'Food's here,' his father announced. 'It's always a bad sign when food arrives that quickly. Probably got it sitting in a vat keeping warm for days.'

'Leonard it'll be fine. I'm sure it'll all be lovely.' She set her face into a smile.

'Lovely,' Mike repeated.

Selected Poems

Rachel Piercey

Truth or dare

These boys are always called
Billy or Finn,

the ones who lead you
into the woods

at just that age
and dare you to eat mushrooms.

I'll swallow whatever you do:
lava discs bursting

from mountains of tree;
white fists

rising out of the dirt.
If you go first.

Close your eyes
and hope he gets it,

your double pledge
of trust

and true love
that licks its lips at death.

The corps

They want to dance Aurora
who unspools
dramatically to the floor

or Odette
who splits herself in two,
or the great rift healer, Juliet.

But privately
the audience likes the corps
most of all, how they spring neatly,

parabola arms exactly
chalked onto the air.
Their careful matching

of dresses, legs and inclined
necks fits the rhythm
of the body inside,

half known and half felt:
the precise, unfurling
geometry of cells.

We recognise
the arc of the two-headed coin
in their eyes –

the acute longing
to be set apart,
the charm of belonging.

Gardening

Late afternoon.
A dusty rhombus of sun
is staking out the shadows.

I've come to pick flowers,
carrying water
to circuit their green wires

immediately,
so they glow in the house
with the same intensity.

I don't know their names
or strange language
of Latin and dirt and tenderness.

I'm at the end of this –
taking them inside,
expecting they'll return next year.

Ride

I

Look, no stabilisers!
I may be cascading
through all the angles of my protractor,
scraping waves into the gravel,
but I'm really going.
And I can always reattach the wheels.

II

Once you might have been a horse
bearing me to lectures, libraries,

tea with friends in postered rooms
overlooking warm quads.

Now I stable you by some railings
on Broad Street, in a grid on St Giles,

or just chain your legs together
and cross my fingers. I got you

in candy pink, to discourage thieves.
I'm sorry I left you behind,

waiting in the college grounds.
I meant to go back and get you.

They wrote saying you would be culled,
it made me think of badgers.

I promise, I did mean to go back.

III

Driving now, boxed up
like a gift to the gods,
I was never so aware
of my own frailty.

At night, I have to get outside.
I ride through
patchy moonlight
and a stew of farm smells,

and in the bright funnel
of visible things
before my handlebars,
droplets arc out

like dolphins
in front of a ship.
I am my whole crew;
I could almost be Triton,

king of my chosen way;
both cresting and part of
the steady undulation,
never having to look back.

Never again

I've been here long enough
that my body
has settled like snow.
There's Strauss in my ears.

The nearest I will get
to what I've always wanted
is in this vaporising
wave of strings.

In the window is the station
where I used to change
for the connecting train.
Now there's no need.

Six months

There's no world yet
where I won't make my arms
into a crib, to line with the silk of her.

The mother takes her back.
Cool air gets to my skin again;
the familiar shock of waking.

A Darkness in the Bones

Katy Tucker

From the novel, Forget Mee Not, *which is written as a book of linked stories telling the life of Amelia Margaret Berry. In the following extract Amelia witnesses the death of her estranged mother.*

'Semolina,' I say. 'She used to love semolina.'
'What the hell is semolina?' asks Rosa.
'It's like...'
'It's revolting,' says Hetty. 'A bowl of sugary sick. Mum used to make us eat it all the time.'
'It's like rice pudding, if it were a puree,' I say.
Hetty presses her lips together to show disgust, still recovering from her rhinoplasty.
Rosa shrugs, uninterested in anything British. My niece is just off the plane from Vietnam, and has been talking about *pho* and mopeds for fifteen minutes. However, Rosa is thirty years younger than us old hags; she has no reason to care about her own country's traditions, yet.
'Well, so, she loved it when we were small. I wonder if you can still get it?'
'Hope not,' says Hetty, and taps something into her tablet-computer. It blinks and returns some search listings. The nurse pops his head into the room, disapproving, and Hetty pretends not to see him. He withdraws, leaving us once again in the half-dark hush of the patients' lounge.
I swill my gritty machine coffee in the too-small cup. 'I thought she might like it now.'
'Pah. She doesn't like anything. Never did.'

Hetty crosses her stalk-like legs. She underwent an operation to cosmetically lengthen her legs years ago, but they botched it: her legs are uneven, the stirrups of her ankles too badly broken to fuse back in their new positions. She doesn't walk easily – not that she ever enjoyed walking – and would simply die, she assures me, if I told anyone about her orthopaedic insoles. She salves her burning shame with the out-of-court settlement of two point six million pounds. It keeps Rosa on the road and Hetty in handsome physiotherapists.

She moves like a colt, now, her skinny, crooked frame weighted down by her heavy boots, as though she would skittle away if she wasn't bound to the floor.

Rosa, tanned and chubby from Vietnamese beef soup and street beer made of rice (or whatever), looks itchy this close to home, crammed back into the mother-child dynamic which suits neither her nor Hetty. She squirms on the waiting-room seat and her curly hair sways, filling the room with its unwashed smell.

In the reception area, a nurse answers a telephone. Rosa has a double chin and I realise she is twenty-six next week. I make a mental note to forbid Hetty from taking her to the cosmetician.

It occurs to me that I do not know what semolina actually is.

'Are you Voirrey's family?' says the nurse. 'You can go back in now.'

*

I put my hand on Rosa's elbow as I guide her down the warm yellow corridor. Yellow makes me think of mother's jaundiced complexion, her poxed body, poisoned by the yellow whiskies she loved.

We step into her stifling room, smothered by the heat.

The cheap alarm clock crunches as it ticks, too loudly, making its unnecessary presence felt. My mother does not need an alarm clock. She does not need to be anywhere but this airless room, among the choking waxy lilies, the sour, soapy smell of bed-washed body.

'Well, this is relaxing,' Rosa says brightly, her youth and health a treason in this room. 'Have you been outside today or are you taking it easy?'

My sallow mother mumbles something, head tucked into the hollow of her chest.

'What was that, Mumsy?' says Hetty. 'Let's lift your bed up.'

With that unsettling judder – everything here happens slowly, too slowly, too loudly in the quiet – the mechanism grinds and heaves and hisses under my mother's weak body, manipulating her spine, uncurling her until her yellow, drooping face is raised towards us. The grey light makes the illness written on her face look like resentment.

Rosa curls up on the chair nearest Granny's head, capable of seeking her own comfort.

'What did you say then, Granny?'

'Nothing about dying is easy.'

Rosa's hand twitches on her grandmother's brow. Just once, but once is enough. Everyone recoils from my mother.

'Has the doctor been in today, Mum?' I say, and am ignored.

'Have you had your lunchtime pills?' Hetty looks at the loud, ugly clock. 'You should probably have had something. Have you had something?'

'Have you had your lunch, Gran?' asks Rosa, softly, gently, from beside my mother's ear. Rosa's voice is that particular pitch of hospice-hush that blazing, aggressive Hetty, and guilty fumbling me cannot master. I am too quiet for my mother – Hetty far, far too loud, saying too many words, like the crunching clock which makes all that noise but cannot make time pass more quickly.

The bed-body mumbles 'Yes, I had peas.'

'Peas? That's nice, Granny. What did you have them with?'

'Peas,' wheezes the old, old woman in the bed, forming milky, washed-out sounds, breathing her stale breath on Rosa, who curls closer. I look at my bitten nails, trying not to feel jealous as my mother (the woman who could not bear to speak to us for years, the woman who chose to be with a bottle instead of us graduating, marrying, divorcing) fights to draw enough breath to rasp meaningless words to Rosa. 'But they wouldn't let me.'

'What wouldn't they let you have, Gran?' Rosa looks over her head at the medical chart, studying the blue and green lines. 'You can have anything you want.'

Hetty tosses her hair and stands up, hobbling too quickly over to the window.

'I wanted...' Mumble. 'I want to go to the toilet.'

Hetty sighs. 'You just went to the toilet, Mum. You went before and that's why we all had to go to the patients' lounge, to give you some privacy, remember?' She mutters the rest so that our mother can't hear. 'Although you've no trouble with pissing in front of the fucking nurses.'

Rosa shoots her an accusing look. I can hear the tea-trolley rattling along the corridor.

'I do *not* remember.' My mother's voice is clipped, *hers* again, and I am part-relieved, part-irritated. In these moments I see that she still is the woman she always was, instead of fearing that our years of fighting were a waste. I imagine this is how defenders feel after long sieges, when the attackers make their first muster in years, reminding everyone why we needed all those fortifications.

But, when she does speak – when she does show herself again – it is hard to believe she isn't putting all this vulnerability on.

'Yes, Granny, you went a moment ago, and that's when I came in and I met Mum and Aunty Amelia in the patients' lounge.'

'Don't lie to me, you – fat – bitch. Get away from me. Get out.'

Her knuckles bulge and shine as she grips Rosa's hand in the thrill of resurrection. Rosa gasps and pulls her arm away from the yellow talons, with four bony stripes imprinted on the young, tanned flesh.

'Don't be a bloody fool.' Hetty stomps out of the room.

'Good afternoon, Mrs Berry,' trills the canteen assistant, clattering into the room, bringing with her wafts of watery coffee and week-old marzipan. 'And how are you today?'

'I want to go to the toilet,' my mother complains, falling limp and weak, disappearing behind her mirage of invalidism.

'Oh, alrighty then. Well we've got your lovely family here to help you, haven't we?'

'I think she'd rather I get a nurse.' I say. The tea-lady looks up at me, startled by my coldness, by my unwillingness to shoulder the burden of the elderly mother who has selflessly wiped my backside and tended to my needs. Under her plain, clean, homely surprise, I shy away and leave. Rosa, bruised and humbled by rejection, slinks out behind me.

*

And now we are back in the waiting room, as the biggest, burliest nurse goes in to minister my mother's ablutions. Poor Violetta – one of the few whose names I know – she must see so many old, decaying anuses. I wonder if Violetta still recognises the sad, slumped scrotum and withered vaginas as sexual organs; maybe she can't switch off, maybe she can't bring herself to wash her own young, functional anus when she gets home.

Mother does not want to go to the toilet; she just wants a break, from waiting for death.

'She's always been fucking cracked in the head,' spits Hetty, crashing the too-small coffee cups in the sink. 'Only now we're supposed to feel sorry for the crazy bitch.'

'Don't you?'

'Don't I?' she shrieks, snatching the cup from the counter and brandishing it at me. 'I feel sorry for us, traipsing round *this shithole* for months on end, paying out of our *arses* to keep her alive when she doesn't even want to be. Let her die, for fuck's sake, don't just pump her full of shite and – *peas*.'

I have heard this before. I take the cup from her slim hands, her beautiful acrylic nails, and the handle breaks off in my grip. The cup drops to the floor, scattering ceramic shards over the lino.

Violetta bustles into the kitchen.

'Oh, what a mess, don't you worry, I'll sort this out.' She barges Hetty out of the way. I press myself against the sink as she sweeps up the broken pieces more capably than I could have. She prattles as she works. 'Your mammy looks bad today, I know, but they always go up and down, these ones, especially with the cancer, they get good and bad days.' She drops the last of the cup-chips in the bin and puts a fat hand on my shoulder.

'Did your mammy know somebody called Viv? An auntie, perhaps, or a teacher?'

I am caught off guard, and look at her blankly.

'She was talking to me like I was old Viv. Old Viv, she said, I never touched a drop after you told me not to. She said Viv, I looked after those girls, I never drank again.'

Hetty has her fingers pressed against her lips so hard that each of her sharp nails is digging into her skin. Her eyes are narrowed, glistening.

Violetta's plump fingers squeeze my cold, thin shoulder. Her breath is sweet, coffee and mints. 'You see, you think she's gone, but she's not gone yet.'

She pats me on the arm, mothering old me, comfortable in her assumption that we cry because we are losing a loved one, when the truth is we lost her years ago.

'No, she's not gone yet.'

The Excursion

Mary Chamberlain

From the opening section of the novel

Phyllis stepped down from the train in her court shoes and the new suit that Grandmother's tailor had made.
'Now you're almost a grown up,' she had said. 'Old enough to marry.' Sneered, 'Though why you chose to go to Girton, and not to the Palace, is beyond me.'
Cor, girl, remembered words from an empty past, *you're as good as any man.*
Dusky skin suited green, the tailor had said, holding the soft tweed to her face, draping it so, polite around the *dusky* word, eyes tip-toeing to Grandmother, a little dark herself from the chin down, where the Yardley's powder stopped.
The station master blew his whistle. Nodded at Phyllis, looked at her squint. Phyllis was used to it, like they never seen *dark* before. *Head high* and look like you know where you're going. She stepped across the track, into the road, opened her handbag and tucked her return ticket into the vanity compartment. *Rislea to Cambridge.*
The mild morning in the gardens of Girton turned raw in the vast steppe of the fen. Wind blew winter from the arctic and angry clouds swelled with rain. Phyllis wished she'd worn her heavy coat and boots. The station road was sodden and rutted. Her heels twisted on their sides. Mud tugged at her shoes, squelched over the sides, planting her feet in the soft, black soil. The train home was not until four o'clock. The road was empty. Houses sulked at its side, not a soul to liven its bleak expanse. The street twisted as if gusts of wind had pulled it this way and that. She wished she hadn't come, no longer knew why she was here.
The rambling street gave way to a green, and to its right, some rickety steps which led down into a dip. Below her Phyllis could see dishevelled rooftops with crooked, yellow smoke straggling from their chimneys. She held the metal railings, took cautious steps on the uneven treads, until she reached the bottom of the hollow. Its chalky sides formed the backs of the dozen or so rough cottages

which had been hewn from the same stone, caves dug out of a hillside. *Troglodytes,* she thought. There was an old-fashioned water pump in front of the houses. Sharp lines hewn into the sides above the roofs formed deep scars in the clunch. Of course, this had had once been a quarry, its marks still visible.

Clunch. She *knew* what the quarry had held. *Clunch.*

The pits were - Phyllis paused. *Pits.* She had called them *pits.* She walked towards the water pump where the runaway had made the soil a quagmire. Rivulets ran out into frothy brown puddles, formed eddies in the ruts. Her smart brown shoes let in water. She backed away, to the haven of the steps. There was a street sign at the top which she hadn't noticed when she went down.

The Pits. This rough place had a familiarity she couldn't grasp. She had been here before, she was sure.

She pulled up the collar of her jacket, and held down her hair which was blowing in the gusty wind. She was cold. Drops of rain began to fall, bubbles in the puddles which *plopped* and rippled.

There was a church ahead. Shelter, of sorts. Phyllis pushed open the lychgate, walked past the antique yews and tombstones to the porch. Fugues and cadenzas were blasting out through the joins and cracks of the ancient building, across the flat ocean of land and echoing round the great cupola of burly sky. A service. She looked at her watch. Midday. It was a bit late. Choir practice.

As she opened the door, the thick, velvet harmonies soared on full, white wings, like archangels entering heaven.

Phyllis stopped, stood.

The church was empty, save for a dumpy woman standing by the baptismal font in a long, brown man's overcoat. She had tied string round its middle, making a crease between her bosom and bottom. She wore a grey trilby hat. Even from this distance Phyllis could see its felt had been mottled by rain and its crown softened by time. Its brim hung wayward and flabby. Shafts of partridge and pheasant plumes spiked from the faded side ribbon which clung by a single thread. A snapshot, no more, flashed in Phyllis's mind. *A trilby hat and the spiky spines of feathers.* And was gone.

The woman had not seen her. She opened her mouth again and a fanfare that would have opened the gates of heaven itself blasted out, sucking in the old oak door with its force and slamming it shut.

The woman stopped, stared at Phyllis.

'Only I like to sing,' she said, as if she'd just left off talking and was picking up the conversation again. 'But not with vicar. I don't hold with his Jesus. So I do it *after*. Just me and *my* God. *He* understand.'

The woman was wearing man's shoes and Phyllis could see the cuffs of her trousers beneath the frayed hem of the old tweed coat.

'I know you,' the woman said. Her voice had an odd timbre, neither low nor high and Phyllis wasn't sure now whether she was a man or a woman.

Phyllis stood, feet together, stiff back, two hands on her handbag in front of her.

'I don't think so.' Yet there was something uncanny about this woman, if that's what she was, smatters of an intimacy that puzzled and disgusted Phyllis.

'You're Meg Goodchild's girl.'

'You're mistaken,' she said. 'That's not my name.'

'Ain't many like you growed up here,' the woman went on, ignoring Phyllis, 'off-white and that. You come wet-eye to me when the others unfair you and I used to take you in. You don't remember so?'

Phyllis shook her head, lips set in an of-course-not expression.

'You scrub me out then?'

She stepped towards Phyllis. Close up, she had two long hairs on one side of her chin, and more on the other side. She sucked in her lips as far as she could, and chomped, whiskers wobbling. Phyllis breathed in her scent of wool and damp and sweat while a powdery moth, light as memory, brushed her nose and flew away.

'Phyllis,' the woman said. 'You name Phyllis.'

The church was cold, but it wasn't the draught that made Phyllis shudder.

'How do you know that?' Her voice was sharp, but it caught at the end, a bidding prayer.

'Like I say,' the woman said. 'I knows you. You named after the fens. Greenery. That's what Phyllis mean.'

She sat down on the bench, patted the side for Phyllis to join her, sidled along to the middle so Phyllis had room.

Phyllis placed herself at the edge of the pew, its tall arm pressing her hip, as far away from the woman as she could. The woman was repulsive in her filthy clothes and man-sized shoes, yet Phyllis couldn't leave, did as she said as if compelled, fear and excitement boxing in her stomach. *Clunch. Pits.* Now this person. She could hear the woman's breathing, *crrrr crrr,* and the bench creak as she fidgeted.

Phyllis stared up at the wooden ceiling with its carved angels and coats of arms, at the soaring windows and empty niches, at the flagstones on the floor, *hic iacet sepultus... requiescit in pace... anno domini....*

'So why you come here then?' The woman said. 'If you ain't coming back?'

If I ain't coming back.

'Seems a person forget she-self round here,' the woman went on. 'Like the wind blow out her sense and *plop* it in the dyke and the water wash it away. But sooner or later that memory pop up like a trout for a fly and a person want to know.'

Phyllis wasn't sure she understood. She fiddled with her gloves, pulling and pushing the soft calf's leather over her fingers, nerves taut, mouth dry.

Rislea. A reason.

'What's your name?' She asked, for want of anything better to say.

'Edie,' the woman said. 'Edie Goddard. But round here, they call me the *he-she* woman. They think I don't know, but I know everything. See – '

Watch out, the he-she woman's behind you.

A flash.

Barefoot children and scabby noses.

The memory flaked away before Phyllis could touch it. The woman shuffled along the bench close to her.

'See, I owns houses,' Edie said. 'I rents them. You gets to know. Every little secret. Who in work. Who ain't.'

She warmed to her theme. 'Friday rent day. Fly, some of them. Send the girl child to answer the door. "Mum ain't home." But I see them through the hinge-crack. I say "Tell your Mum she owe me. I ain't charity." Onliest person who pay on time, and honest, was your mother.'

Phyllis's mind soared. Cheeks burned. Dizzy. She faced Edie.

'My mother? You knew my mother?'

Edie chewed her lip, chin hairs bobbing.

'You forgotten your own mother?' Edie said, but her voice was soft, not spiteful. She put a red, crinkled hand over Phyllis's fingers, smooth in soft, tan leather.

'I reckon that's why you come back. After all these years. How old you was when you left? Seven? Eight? It was in the war, that's for sure.'

Mother's vest. She had taken it then, put it on over her own, under her dress, so no-one would see, kept it all those years, wrapping herself in her mother's sweat, snuffling in its love and warmth. She'd rubbed her head too, where her mother's tears had moistened her hair, and the damp left must in her nostrils.

'See,' Edie said. 'Everybody has to have a story. A beginning and a end. Else we don't know ourself. We just meat and bone otherwise, *searching* for what makes us *different*, me from you.'

Edie chomped, grunted, took off her trilby hat and scratched her hair. It was thinning, like a man's.

Phyllis had a story. Grandmother gave it to her, cut it to fit, suited her complexion. *It's best you forget. This is your home now.* Phyllis did forget.

But the husks of memory stayed. She had run her fingers through their dust and toyed with their floating shells, blowing them until her hands were empty. Every night she had pressed the ageing cloth to her nose, its scent long since worn away, knowing that comfort lay buried in the fetid wool.

'I ain't use to visitors,' Edie was saying. 'But I got a fire, and the house is warm, and I could tell you a thing or two on your mother. And your father.'

'You knew him too?'

Her father's tickets, buried in the lining of the old trunk.

'Oh yes,' Edie said. 'I got the measure of him and all.'

She scratched her head again and put her hat back on. Phyllis pushed herself up from the pew, followed Edie out of the door.

Selected Poems

Anna Kirk

Breakfast

He was lax with the razorblade,
now they eat eggs.
Ted chews his toast and stares so hard
he can see into his mouth.
Sylvia takes the butter knife and busies herself
with triangles.
Silence but for soft bites.
She looks at him and there's a finger
in her eye.
He's going for sleep's leftover,
marmalade coloured.
Ted stares at the crust stuck to his nail tip
as if he had been panning for gold
and has found a nugget.
She feels the glow from it.

Janet and John

I read lesbian Bildungsromane
as you read Renaissance
Revenge Tragedies. My edition
is trashy with two naked women
fondling inside a flower on the
front. Your dramatis personae
span pages so we roll names
on our tongues. I underline all
references to fruit as you dose off
fathoming murder plots. I used to
make Dada poems out of nonsense
words, burrow my bones into cotton
I warmed with myself. Now I read
in the crook of your arm, the cave
of your chest, all words are
nonsense.

Scalp Hunter

After Rosemary Tonks

You are clothed in fresh wounds stitched together with
hairs that are forever on the cusp of grey; a dress
peach skin to touch, the colour of sucked plums. You brew
parfait amour by bleaching love-in-idleness – blood clot
petals in cut glass tumblers. Your index finger feels
for scent around the rim and dabs the fingerprint dew
behind your ears. You are a scalp hunter! breath stealer!
– collecting all the names you ink into your dance card.
men's eyes roll inside their heads. They reel! and you slice
away loose skin. You show skulls the heavens – skulls
like gibbous moons, bone doused in carmine. Soft crowns
(tight-knit only after birth) take in the open air, unprotected.

You are a scalp hunter though they say you are a vampire.
Two cicatrix, magnolia pale with new tissue long grown over,
are glimpsed an inch from your throat in good light. They say
you were bitten by man. But you know better… The marks are
scars from childhood chicken pox. You scratched.

Sweet Tooth

She took it for herself. He did not use it any more
and she was hungry for it.
She keeps it in the stronghold of her cheek, tonguing it,
worrying it, fending off rot.
It is her sharp and polished tool.

She gives it back as they finish dessert,
folding napkins into boats.
She watches him fix his old tooth back into its hole,
all gum clumsy,
while her folds of flesh birth her own sweet tooth.

Romantics

Summer brings a bout of pregnant women
with its heat and storms unsolicited.
Under a shared umbrella we walk

through a graveyard, St Pancras Old Church,
where first they lay together, Percy
and Mary, mixing soil with sin.

We find it difficult to finish sentences,
so we wrap them up in manuscript paper
sealed with lips half open.

Thin ink scratched Mary's wanting diary entry
'Find my baby dead. A miserable day'.
Wash the blood away with rain

just as we brush our teeth each night,
unfinishing our sentences.

Binary

He primarily works with numbers. He writes
programmes for computers. He builds them
using text-book codes he then revises,
rearranges, edits into something that can
hum. He reads the ones and noughts
until they become the poetry of Shakespeare.
Nought becomes O. Not a nothing but a code
for rapture, despair, lust, woe.
The O he reads is filled in,
a hole in the screen, holding everything.
He names the computers on his home
network after favourite characters from
A Midsummer Night's Dream. Quince,
Puck, Titania. He types directly into Oberon.

The Strawberry Thief

Laura McClelland

September 1874. May Morris, 12-year-old daughter of designer and poet William Morris, has spent the summer at Kelmscott Manor in Oxfordshire with her mother Janey and sister Jenny – and her mother's lover, the painter poet Dante Gabriel Rossetti. Morris has made his escape to Iceland and, during his absence, May has begun to bloom, as has her friendship with Gabriel.

Morris's return signals the end of summer for all of them. As the grown-ups set about tying their own lives in knots, and with the ever present threat of her sister's spiralling ill health, May needs to decide if she is ready to take the next step to becoming a grown-up herself. Set against the backdrop of the artist's studio at Kelmscott and the Morris and Co firm in London, will she be able to decide whether or not she wants to be caught?

The fall was too quick. Water dark like the tunnel inside an eye, opens wide to let Jenny in then closes its lids to hold her tight. May can remember it, every few seconds it happens again. The blankness spreading across Jenny's face like relief as she dips back into the water, as if falling is the obvious thing to do. May opens her eyes into the safe taut linen of the pillow but she cannot stay awake, sleep and the memory pull her under and Jenny is slipping away again and again.

Father is the one to send the boat spinning, now he is in the water and for a moment she and Mother cannot see anything, they have been sent the wrong way. They turn back, but there is only froth and movement on the surface and nothing, for a second there is nothing below.

It had been a good day, one of the last ones before Father went to Iceland. They'd been alone on the Thames, the London bit, just the four of them. *No non-Morrises allowed*, Father had said, spreading his oars wide.

She and Jenny were allowed to roll up their skirts and dangle bare legs from the riverbank. Their feet bobbed pink like salmon in the shadowy water. In the boat there were strawberries with white sugar to sprinkle, they each had their own bottle of ginger beer.

Mother had a headache and a parasol. Father was explaining something and she was leaning forward to listen, trying to angle the parasol to keep the clean bright surface of the water from her thoughts. That was as far as they'd got, the row to the middle of the river, that was the end of the memory of Jenny still in the boat.

May leans out to where Father must be, with Jenny. She can feel the nearness of the water, it is a thing turned bad, against them. She is aware of it, like a gaze on the back of her neck. She parts the water with her hands, as if she can prise it open and make a hole for Father to pull Jenny out. Mother is doing the same beside her, they splash and there is the taste of city water, sharp and grey on her lip.

A single drop of water flies at a different angle to the rest, this one comes from outside the boat. It lands on a wooden board at her feet, which is already soaked, but she can see this droplet, it is separate. She tries to remember why.

Coughs follow the water and there is Father with Jenny, he holds her with two arms like a trophy, it is only his face that is missing the triumph. May pulls at the water and eventually there is something there to hold on to, a piece of cloth that could be connected to Father or Jenny, she doesn't care so long as she can pull.

Sheets wind around her fingers, they are slippery with river-water or sweat. Jenny is staring straight at her, from inside the border of Father's arms she looks peaceful. It is Mother beside May who is sending out panic enough to engulf them all. Father lifts Jenny and Jenny kicks, river scum leaves her feet and attaches to Father, there is algae on his face, he will ignore it and it will dry and become a part of him, until someone comes at him with a wet cloth. He will make everyone tend to Jenny, if they can get her out.

May tries to stay with them, but there is something on the bank and she wants to see what it is. She tries to turn her head and look at it directly, but when she does there is nothing but bare ground. She is almost back to Jenny when it is there again, glittering in the corner of her eye. It is a dark thing, an animal but she is not sure which. The glitter must be from its eyes, from the water moving beneath them, because the animal, she is sure, is sitting still. Its hide is black, a wet fur of some kind, or a scale. It is watching Jenny, everything about it is focussed on the distress in the river, but it is calm, it does not seem to mind.

The slap of water being struck sounds behind her and May turns back. Jenny's kicks are more desperate now and May feels her own feet struggling to kick in unison. She has been caught by something, she jerks her legs in frustration but she cannot get them free. She needs to lean out, to help keep hold of Jenny, just a little further and the ends of her fingers will be touching.

May woke, her body was half out of the bed, diving towards the floor. Her feet were held in place by a tangle of bedclothes, they had saved her from the plunge. She let her body hang in the air for a minute and kept her eyes on the wooden boards below, not looking up at the glitter and the darkness. Four wet paws, damp and black with fur, were waiting for her on the other side of the room.

*

Blood. May woke again, damp with new sweat over the layer that had dried in the night. Something was new. She lay still until she knew what it was. She ran her mind over each part of her body feeling for the problem. Warm dull limbs, rosy angles. New air in the down of her arm. Barely damp sweat in the bend of her neck. She concentrated. Something was drawing her down. There was something sticky between her legs.

She knew what it was - the thing Gabriel had told her about. She wasn't clear about why it happened, or why now. Gabriel hadn't got that far, maybe he didn't know. She tried to feel for whatever was working inside but there was nothing, as if it wasn't really her blood.

Until she stood up, it wasn't too bad. There was the patch on the mattress. That was almost dry. She found a matching stain on the back of her nightdress. She didn't really mind that either. She tried to think about how the blood had spread through the cloth, to see the pattern. Red, crust, white.

It was the three small drops of blood that fell when she stood.

She watched them land between her feet. Wet and new. Part of her on the floor. She hadn't noticed at first that there was pain, slight, aching. Just beginning to become something else.

She crouched to examine the drops and more fell where she crouched. Three, four, five perfect raised discs. Dark, almost brown against the wood, they didn't spread. It would have been better if they'd run together in a little wet track, but they stayed separate. May glanced across at Jenny who was still sleeping as if nothing was wrong. Sickness clutched at May's stomach, because Jenny's breaths were calm and steady, like the river against the earth of the bank. It was too steady, too calm. She was bleeding and she was the only one who knew.

With her palm, May wiped away the blood. It left a smear, so she cleaned her hand against her nightdress and did it again. This time she could hardly see it. She tested it with her foot, checking her toes for traces of blood. She didn't want to leave footprints outside, for Jenny to find when she woke. Father was coming home, this was supposed to be a good day.

May got as far as the landing before her feet asked for direction. She stood on the spot to think, but lightly, keeping the weight out of her heels and so out of the rug below. Gabriel would still be asleep and besides, she knew without thinking that this was something to keep hidden. She sighed. Mother.

She tiptoed down the landing, not wanting to dislodge any more blood. Mother was going to be cross already, it would be worse if she found blood in the hall. The thought of Mother began to bloom, giving out tiny shoots of satisfaction that throbbed in May like swollen veins. She would be the same as Mother now.

One of the shoots wound itself too tightly around her inside, aiming for light but instead burrowing deeper. She would be the same as Mother now.

She knocked on Mother's door. It was early but there was something about the quiet in the house that made her think she wasn't the only one awake.

'Gabriel?'

Mother's voice was tired, as if determined not to be curious.

'Mother, it's me.'

'Jenny? Are you all right?' This time the voice was quick and fearful.

Behind the door, footsteps hurried and May braced herself, next moment she would be discovered not to be Jenny at all.

The door swung and there was Mother, lit with anxiety, her cheek brushed with concern. She saw May and her skin paled again, the rose in her cheeks sank beneath the surface and relief and disappointment came and went and were replaced with blankness. May saw it all and swallowed. She wasn't Jenny.

'Oh, May.'

Mother's breath quickened again, relapsing fear. 'There's nothing wrong with Jenny is there?'

'She's fine.' May's hand slid towards Mother, she felt it reaching out of her control. It lay itself on Mother's forearm, where Mother stared down at it too.

'She's still asleep,' May said.

'Oh. Thank goodness.'

Mother turned back to her room, retreated. May's hand was left behind, waiting, as if Mother's arm would return. The door was open so May followed her inside, but quietly.

'It's me.'

'Yes, I know,' Mother seemed as if she didn't know.

'No, I mean it's me that there's something the matter with.'

'Oh yes?'

Mother was looking out at the morning, through the window. In her fingers, a thin cord from the curtain tie twisted itself into knots.

Silence & Shadows

Viv Graveson

As Beatrice and her older sister Flora grow up in pre-war London, their differences drive them apart. Flora's life revolves around her family and the River Thames where her hero-father works as a lighterman. Beatrice dreams of escape to Paris. However, as they reach adulthood, the reality of WW2 hits and they are forced to rethink their lives.

Flora, now married, leaves for the safety of the country with baby Annie, and Beatrice stays, relishing the danger of the Blitz. But when her officer-lover is killed fighting in France, she seeks comfort from William, an old friend, and finds herself pregnant with his child. She turns to Flora for help. Little does Beatrice realise this will set in train a series of events that will break Flora's heart and estrange the sisters forever.

In 2002, after Beatrice's death, daughter Delphine, receives a letter from her mother's wartime past. Perhaps she can at last begin to unravel the mystery that has haunted their lives.

The extract is from Chapter 4 as Flora is beginning to get to know her father again after he has come home wounded from the Great War.

1919

It appeared out of nowhere, a flagpole, shiny and bright, its top lost in a haze of sky. Such a grand thing, brighter and newer than anything else around. Flora's eyes hurt to look at it.

Her mother had a fist on each hip and was staring up too. Pearls of rain from the lupins brushed onto her overall and glistened before fading into the fabric.

'What've you gone and got that for?' Mother demanded.

'I thought I might sit on top of it?' said Father.

'Hummph,' she said crossly.

One of his eyebrows dipped in a wink and Flora giggled. On the ground, leaning against the pole's base, was the sandy-coloured satchel he used for his sandwiches. It was spotted with dark from the earlier rain, and blades of grass stuck out from where it had squashed them. Bending, he reached in his long fingers, drew out a brown paper package and handed it to Flora.

It was heavy.

'Go on,' he said, 'open it.'

She looked at him uncertain and he nodded. The paper was stiff and crackly and difficult to unwrap. She bent to lean it against her knee. Whatever happened, it mustn't fall. Slowly, she peeled back the paper.

'Give it here.'

When he shook it out, she knew what it was. A Union Jack. He held it up high in front of him like a sheet. It made the lupins and pinks disappear.

'What do we want with one of those?' her mother asked, but she was smiling now.

'You'll see, by and by.'

Flora watched as he refolded the flag. He did it carefully, keeping to the creases already there. When he held out his hand for the paper, Flora gave it to him and he wrapped the flag back inside.

'Sometimes, Nathaniel Walker, you go beyond yourself,' said her mother. Flora didn't think he'd heard. Already he was hobbling up the path to the kitchen. She stood for a moment and then followed him into the house.

He was waiting for her, his fingers on the handle of one of the dresser drawers.

'Now you know where it's kept,' he said.

Flora looked at him. It was as if he was recruiting her, making her his ally. She kept her smile hidden inside.

From the doorway, came her mother's voice: 'Get along slack-Alice, some of us've got work to do.'

For many weeks the flagpole stayed bare, just a tall white strip reaching up and up into a dot against the clouds. The words for asking about it burned inside her. But she waited, quiet and patient, and when he wasn't looking, checked the drawer to see if the parcel was still there, smoothing her hand over the shiny brown paper.

Then, one day, a bright and windy Sunday in August, her daddy beckoned her to his battered green chair by the window. His pipe clicked against his teeth and when he sucked in his cheeks, she could hear the bubbling sound inside. In the bowl at the end, the tobacco glowed red.

'Go and get the flag then, girl,' he said. The pipe bobbed up and down. 'You remember where it is?'

Flora nodded.

There it was, safely in its drawer.

She pulled out the parcel and turned. He had followed her in, was there at her side.

'Well?'

She held it out. A page before her king.

'Put it on the table.'

But his watching was making her stiff, the sound of his breathing along with the *suck-suck* noise of his pipe filling the room. She felt heavy and awkward. Her fingers fumbled and, for a second, she thought the paper would tear. Then the fabric slid from its wrappings and onto the bleached grey wood.

'You can open it up if you want.'

She shook it and the colours billowed out. Her father caught the other end and they held it together. It was big, bigger than the table and the chairs around it, filling the scullery nearly.

'That thing belongs in the garden,' her mother's voice said from the stairs.'

'This is called the "alyard", see,' he said when they'd made their way down past the summer-drooping flowers and the outhouse with its hot, sour smell. He indicated the twine he was threading through the openings on the side of the flag.

'Alyard,' said Flora.

'That's it.'

She looked up. Beyond the fading lupins, her mum was watching from the window. Flora waved and she smiled and nodded her head.

'Right oh, corporal,' said her daddy, and her heart leapt. 'Time to hoist the flag.'

The handle was stiff and awkward and hurt her fingers. She pressed her lips together and leaned harder into the task, curving her back. Slowly the Union Jack creaked its way upward. Flora stopped for a breath and jumped as her father's long fingers closed over hers, the hard dry bits from his work on the lighters digging into the back of her hand. She could smell only the boats and the river. A thrilling mixture of oil and timber and tar. Together, they turned the handle and guided the flag to the very top of the mast.

Heads craned back, they watched as it flattened itself against the wind.

It was wonderful.

'Do you know what today is, my girl?' her father asked.

Flora shook her head.

'Today,' he said in a solemn voice, 'is the anniversary of the Battle of Wipers.'

Flora knew it had something to do with the war. The war that had kept her daddy away from her for so long. She knew, too, that she was supposed to look sad when grown-ups talked about it. So she stood up properly, pulling her shoulders back like she'd seen the soldiers do, and looked at her father with her very serious face on. But what she felt inside was different, a mixture of butterflies deep in her tummy and happiness.

This was because raising the flag was the very best thing that had happened since her daddy had come back.

He was her friend now. Which was what she wanted more than anything.

Every Sunday after lunch, as long as her father was not out on the river, they had their 'drill'. That was when Flora carried the carefully folded flag past the bedraggled flowerbeds and the dustbin and the vinegary-smelling privy, to where he was waiting by the flagpole. Her nose stuck in the air and her aching arms up high, she walked so that even the leaves, which might have snails on them or still be wet from the rain, were no threat to it.

She knew he did the drills to please her. Like before when she'd been little and he'd put her on his shoulders or held her hand. But it wasn't enough. Each time she found herself asking, 'Can we put the flag up properly today?'

And each time, he said, 'No, ducks, that wouldn't be right. It's to commemorate the battles. This is just practice.'

She began to count the weeks.

There were a lot of them. They stretched out past the beginning of the school term, past the days when they started to learn fractions, and into the lengthening, wind-bitten nights of autumn.

After the eighth Sunday, she said, 'When can we do it? Isn't there a battle soon?' and looked at him with pleading eyes.

He regarded her silently, his expression dark. Sounds drifted down from the top of the yard. Her mother emptying something into the drain behind the scullery. The clatter of a bucket. She knew if she looked away, he wouldn't reply.

'A child your age,' he began at last, but his voice was cold. 'Should be out playin'.'

Tears pricked in an instant. She fought them back.

'But I'm your corporal,' she said, determined to take the full force of his gaze. 'You said so.' The words broke through trembling lips.

For a moment he seemed not even to breathe. He twisted away and stared hard at the ground. When he turned, what his face said didn't frighten her anymore. Her heart began to beat again.

'I don't deserve you,' her father said quietly.

She looked down, not knowing. He handed her back the flag and she hugged it to her chest.

'Tell you what, Corporal,' he said, forcing cheerfulness. 'We'll raise it for the Battle of Cambray. That's December. What d'yer think?'

She felt almost weightless with relief. But even so, December was a very long way away from October. December was Christmas.

She nodded anyway. 'Yes please.'

'That's when we stopped Jerry getting their supplies!' he said.

It was the first time he'd ever really talked about the war. She stood very still.

'Gave 'em a turn, I can tell you.'

'Is that where you were – at Cam... at that Cam place?' she asked carefully.

He wound the rope around the wooden pegs and stepped back, peering down at her from his great height.

'I wasn't there, ducks. No. I was somewhere else.' He hesitated for a moment. 'I'm not sure it's right to talk about these things – they're not for kiddies' ears. But it was a big battle – with tanks.' His eyes were wide at the thought of it.

She hardly dared breathe.

'They'd never seen nothin' like it,' he said.

It was as if he'd opened a door to a space she didn't know and invited her in. She must take very small steps.

'So we were the winners?'

'No-one won really,' her father said quietly. 'War's not a good thing, Flora. Men get killed.'

'But not you?' Her voice was a whisper.

'No, not me.'

'Is it where Uncle Ernie died?'

Another step.

'No. He was somewhere else. It was called "The Somme".'

'Oh.' Flora scratched at the ground with her foot. The Somme was a bad place. 'Can we say a prayer,' she said finally, 'to God. For the soldiers.'

His face closed; she'd gone too far. His eyes moved somewhere beyond her look. 'If God 'ad wanted to help 'em,' he said bitterly, as if to a stranger, he'd have done it at the time.'

She bit her lip. Sometimes it was really hard.

Longing

Barney Norris

From Chapter One

'Sean!'

He looked back up the field, his view half obscured by bleached stalks, egret-shinned, and saw his mother standing by the broken down stile. Her hands were full of sloes, thin light quavering behind her in the white clouds flooding the sky over her head. She was almost silhouetted where she stood, he could barely make out the details of her face.

'Are you coming back?'

'In a minute.'

'Will you come back for your tea?'

'Yes.'

'Will you?'

He tried to smile, but he wanted her to leave him alone, and knew it showed. The way he didn't turn his body to face her, didn't come home when she asked him. She stood there in her old clothes, slumped shoulders, looking like nobody had ever loved her, and waited for his answer.

'Yes.'

Rose looked down at her son, kneeling at the edge of the wheat field, a stalk half flayed in his hand and a hole by his right foot where he had been digging into the ground with his heel. The darker earth he had scraped up was scattered around him, still wet with secrecy, like a great mole had thrown it off. He would get soil all over his trousers.

'What are you doing?'

'Nothing. Digging.'

'Digging?'

'Yeah.'

'Don't make a mess. I'll see you in a bit, all right?'

She turned away and started back home to cook the tea, stepping past the stile through the gap in the hedge, then walking fast and head-down along the bridlepath. She had worn the wrong shoes to come this far. She didn't know why she bothered anyway, he didn't want to spend time with her. Now she had her hands full of sloes, and she couldn't shield her face from the brambles hanging across the way. She was afraid they would whip at her eyes, catlike, vindictive. A hundred yards along the lane she gave up and dropped the berries into the hedge, angry at herself for picking them, furious she had to let them go, then walked on with one arm up to cover her face. She had only turned away for a minute, distracted by the sloes, thinking how John had loved the gin she used to make out of berries picked from these hedges, and Sean was digging a hole with the heel of his good school shoes. She should have made sure he was wearing his plimsolls before they left the house. None of his things seemed to last as long as they should.

Sean was a distant, thoughtful boy, happy to spend his days on his own. Salisbury and the fields around were a good place to pass them. If you walked for fifteen minutes in any direction you found yourself more or less out of the town. Beyond were big fields and song birds and trees and rivers that took up most of his time. Trespassing in woods, he watched hedgehogs, deer and hare and badgers doing their rounds through ground elder and the shoots that grew on the floor of deciduous woodland. He walked in bluebells, loving the smell, though he never had anyone to pick them for. Apart from his mother, but he never brought any home for her. Once, to see what it felt like, he ran in shorts and t-shirt through a ditch of nettles, and thought afterwards that he might die as he lay down on a mowed grass bank, scent of the new-cut grass like a sea rising round him, to experience a burning vivid as the colour of a flower.

On his walks, he learned the names of trees and plants, and the calls of birds so he could imitate them, though he never imitated them very well. He noted down in frayed exercise books he titled 'Camping' what flowers came out where and when, that the texture of a leaf was different in March and in summer, that a fern in the spring curled round the air like it had fallen in love with it. He filled several books with these observations, with notes about himself, bad poems, the lives of the people he was getting away from when he came out into the woodland and scrub. He stole the books from unguarded stationery cupboards at school. Then, once he was alone, he sat down with them and stared hard at the world around. It told him secrets other people didn't listen to, though they were there for finding all the time, a boy could make them out. He wrote them into the books, and then they would stare up from the page as well. He could take them with him, however far he went from what he thought of as the real world. Mysteries plucked from the hedgerows, from the bramble fingers snaking down.

He knew the coming of spring was first marked by a change in the air. You felt it on your skin – the wind moved differently against your face, as if it was discovering different directions, whirled on a compass. It brought the smell of life with it, new shoots before they opened and the surfaces of ponds or lakes disturbed back into life by the return of migratory birds. Lakes, which all winter had reflected nothing but the ruffling wind, grey palette of the sky, the quiet world asleep and at bay, turned their mirror on the world and found life. The scree of water thrown up by a goose or a duck or a swan when it landed. The worrying of small birds flitting the surface. The birds brought a new light with them, as if trailed after them, a blanket of life drawn over the land that woke the country. You felt it first in the air, then spring arrived as a pale light that eased the winter apart. The whole world opened like a clam. Sean found that out and wrote it down. Once it was in the book he could carry spring with him wherever he went, and every time he opened the book it was spring again.

Sometimes he walked for whole weekends. In the New Forest he tried to track deer, having once spent an afternoon following one through the woods that seemed to be leading him because it refused to bolt. He waded through sucking mud that made claims on his shoes for what seemed like hours, until finally he was stopped in his own tracks by the sight of an adder coiled under bracken at the edge of a stream, which raised its head when it saw him and silently faced him down. Sean had been taught to be afraid of adders, as they were the only thing in England with the venom to kill. Their threat made them fascinating, and he learned and loved the diamond pattern of yellow and blue that marked them out, savouring their Latin name's rhyming sharpness on his tongue, *vipera berus*. He wished he was an adder. He went after deer in the hope they might lead him back to one. But he still knew if he ever saw an adder that he was supposed to be afraid. He had backed away slowly, and looked up to find the deer was gone.

Or he could go north out of the city, onto the bare expanses of Salisbury Plain or to Old Sarum, the hill fort site of the original settlement at Salisbury. He used to climb the outer walls and scale the fence to walk among the ruins of the old castle and cathedral, until the introduction of a souvenir kiosk led to a guard with an Alsatian dog being paid to sit up there in a car after hours, listening to scratchy all-night radio. Sean was caught climbing in and escorted from the premises. He escaped further punishment by doing his best Just William voice. He had noticed long vowels changed the way people were treated.

'I'm on a midnight ramble.'

'You're what?'

The security guard, a boy not much older than Sean, had a Hampshire accent. Sean supposed he must have had to drive some way in to work.

'A midnight ramble.'

'It's half nine.'

'I know. I'm just getting started. I'm sorry I was trespassing, I didn't know. I got lost.'

'Did you?'

'I'm not from round here you see. I'm from Windsor.'

'Windsor?'

'In Chelsea.' He had never been to either of these places, but he knew they were posh. 'I've walked here.'

The security guard raised an eyebrow.

'Have you now. Didn't you think it was getting a bit steep? As you rambled up the outer walls?'

Selected Poems

Lyn Thornton

The Burning

This much I remember. Running out of the house
    my mother shouting after me,
        me whooping through the night to the great
            blaze of a hay stack
                set alight by Ockie Johnson.

They say he fires a stack every year to claim insurance
    but we know different,
        we know it's for some summer god
            whose name we can't pronounce
            although we try.

The heat forces us back, curls the hedgerows
    into black knots. Sparks fly
        though the night sky
        brighter than stars
            small, wide eyed creatures run for their lives.

For five days and nights the great mass smoulders
    the earth bares the stain
        charred forever, or so it seemed then.
        This much I remember.

Waves

    howl like wolves in chains

but today another sound, the slither

of a train entering a station,

        again

            and again,

fear curls our toes in the sand

but the gull doesn't hear it or

        the sandpiper on the shoreline

or the dog chasing the waves;

it echoes behind the rocks, the rush

        of trains meeting

            beneath

                mountains.

A Dead Fish

An eighteenth century Dutch painter
would have caught its perfection,
its stillness, the absorption of
brightness, armorial scales shaded
into night, plump on a pewter platter
its fluidity captured on canvas,
made immortal, at one
with the sea.

Here it is nothing
a fish washed up on a beach
eyes bright, gills open wide,
its last gasp taken.

Viola

A trunk in an attic, a foil
against moths, now spills

its gaudy contents in the light
that captures the rupture of shot silk
before the dust settles; tight velvet
breeches for a loose limbed Viola,
her reward, a promised happy ever after
husband, children, and she, the perfect
wife.

Where are you now, in a jazz café in Zurich
peering out across the lake for a ferry with a green
light?

For G.C.

They say you've moved to Buenos Aires
there you stroll though great arcades
or stumble along uneven pavements
when the light fades. Visit little known
urban churches, feast on familiar Rococo
detail with an architect's eye, watch old
men in cafés playing cards, inhale nicotine
as though taking your last breath.

Perhaps some days you dream of Barcelona
your old apartment with its art nouveau
accoutrements then sink back into this
uneasy restoration making a Guidi
landscape with a fractured mosaic, still
looking for your cathedral of the heart.

White Notley Hall

i

Here there are no stone walls only wattle
and daub lintels and mossed thatch, serpentine
lanes, a Norman church, an Elizabethan manor
house. Visit it in Spring time and see a modesty
of snowdrops tucked deep into the earth where
once Phoenician traders set up shop. Coming up
river from Wivenhoe they laid out their cargo
of spangled glass, silks and pots, long before
the Romans dug out a lake in a fold of land;
claimed this place as home.

ii

Now they are gone
logs still flame in the great hall
rooks still shelter in cedars
as wind rakes the fields.

An acreage of daffodils flouts Spring
daring a heavy sky to shed late hail
molten lead against window panes.

After such absence others light their fires
never noticing the peacock's trail of feathers
over fields of snow.

Gogmagog

There's no good reason why
my pulse quickens when I see
the mist rise on an autumn
morning over the Gogmagog
hills, but it does.

It's best to get there early
when the birds sing out bold
notes and leaves tremble with
moisture as the sun traces patterns
on silver barks, transforms foliage
into strange cosmologies.

As the vapour clears, a late butterfly
stretches, catches the warmth on mossed
wings, rests for a moment on a giant's
curved thigh, exhausted after battle. I hear
his sad exhalation and dream of a time
before mythmaking.

Ophelia's Song

My lover says I'm mad
I know I'm not.

Here's rue for you
and columbine,
rosemary for remembrance.

An old king in an orchard
lay, sleeping. Something
happened, I mustn't say,
Best forgot,
best forgot.

Here's rue for you
and columbine,
rosemary for remembrance.

The stream is flowing
fast today, watch your step
my mother used to say
before the waters
floated her away.

Here's rue for you
and columbine,
rosemary for remembrance.

Keep Your Belief Strong

Rebecca Perl

I was on a bus journey that was jarring my bones, rattling my teeth. The whistling driver overtook into oncoming traffic then swerved onto our side with seconds to spare. After three weeks of travelling in Vietnam I knew this to be normal. Besides, I was too tired to care much. The lady curled up next to me looked like a brown Yoda and smelt of patchouli. In front of me was a man with the expression of a kicked dog, hair parted by spit and a plastic comb. A mother was trying to soothe her baby with the vibration of a low-hummed melody.

Out the window buffalo were grazing next to pylons. The green of the paddy fields with water shimmering underneath was cartoon in its lushness then it was gone, replaced by dust and pock-marked roads. I saw the vague promise of mountains meeting sky, the same shade of duck-egg blue. Rows of shacks doubled as shops and out front tatty flags still managed to look dignified. Through the cloud, through the glass, the sun was building strength. Apart from the mother and whimpering baby, all other passengers were sleeping. Necks wobbled under the weight of rolling heads. Jaws slackened. Chins doubled.

At home, I had made a few attempts at relationships followed by a few attempts at no-strings-attached fun, all of which had resulted in me feeling like shit. I booked the trip to Vietnam to be alone, to get far away from my life. I vowed that no man would be a part of my experience or penetrate my feelings. I was independent. I was an ice queen. I'd done well so far, shunning conversation from perfectly nice characters whose only crime was owning a penis. Of course, I made exceptions for men past a certain age whose penises didn't even enter my consciousness. Such as Bill, the indoor sunglasses wearer who shuffled over to ask if he could join my breakfast table this morning. I knew he was Canadian straight off because he kept saying '*aboot*' perhaps to make sure he wasn't mistaken for an American. All the while he was spearing slices of mango, pineapple and papaya, he was telling me about his magic bus adventures from the sixties and seventies in his monotone stoner drawl.

We stopped for a break, 'happy hour' the driver called it, the chance to piss on a patch of soaked concrete, smoke cigarettes, and eat peanut caramel snacks that would have your teeth out. I was seated, didn't see him approaching.

'Mind if I sit here?' He was already on his way to sitting down as he asked.

A fellow Brit, Londoner I guessed, although everyone south of Watford was a Londoner to me.

'Go ahead,' I said, too late, as he was already seated.

The green chairs were not made for adults of our size. I was all legs at the best of times. Being folded up made me even more self-conscious. I crossed my arms tightly over my stomach as if applying pressure to an open wound. My finger found flesh through a small hole in the seam of my top. Why did he have to sit with me? There were loads of free seats. I hated making conversation. I had grown to be comfortable on my own, looking out at the world and forgetting that people could see in.

We both ordered coffees, which arrived in glasses topped by tin pots. I listened to it dripping through. The coffee was the colour of Guinness. At first, the spoon didn't move freely in the thickness at the bottom of the glass, then gradually became easier and the blackness emerged pale as butterscotch. He didn't appear bothered by our silence. When I couldn't take it any longer, I blurted out, 'The coffee is so good.'

'I'm not surprised. Have you seen how much condensed milk goes into one of these bad boys?'

'And how much coffee. Pretty strong stuff. Almost chewy.'

'That's us up all night then,' he grinned.

An easy, well-used smile. The lines around his eyes told me that. He had a hint of a dimple on his right cheek.

It was raining when the bus arrived. The driver dumped our bags on the pavement with the shit and spit. There was no one to meet us – no one offering a taxi, motorbike, hotel – probably because of the weather. We decided to walk to a guest house I had heard about. He was taller, though not so tall I had to look up. The rain, which felt soft, was driving down at an angle. Within minutes I had wet Converse and soggy jeans. Head down, face contorted into a grimace, I glanced over at him. He ran a hand through his soaked hair and offered his face to the sky.

'We're not made of sugar, you know,' he said, kindly, resting his hand on the nape of my neck for a moment.

'No, I guess not,' I laughed, stepping around deep puddles that would be gone again soon enough.

The next morning I was woken by a knock at my door. Curled in on myself like an animal, I was tangled in unhemmed sheets, the odour of the last unwashed guest ever-present.

'Hang on,' I croaked, wiping the remnants of last night's mascara from under my eyes with a finger.

I pulled the door open just sufficient for my head, not so wide that he could see my stripy vest and blue boxers and arm hairs standing on end.

'Nice do,' he said. His laugh was light.

I knew even before I touched it that my hair was a gravity-defying, insomnia-crafted sculpture.

'Thanks. I try.'

'Want to come to the lake?' he asked, rubbing his head.

'Definitely. I'll meet you downstairs in five.'

I checked my mobile: 6:22am.

The darkness was already paling outside, the streets an empty blue. As the mist rose from the lake, people lined its banks, flinging themselves into the day. An old woman in a floral face mask and a knock-off tracksuit did standing squats, arms outstretched as if to hold back the water. A man used the power of his compact body to propel his high kicks. With each swing, his foot reached the same point of air. He didn't break a sweat. His face was calm, as though he was reading a magazine. On the banks of the west side, a large group danced staccato ballroom to bellowing music. Most were in couples – men and women, men and men, women and women. One lady dressed all in white danced alone, joyfully repeating the same pivot step, over and over. He pointed to the road, at a moving floral spectacle. We could just make out the top of a hat, barely visible among the clusters of magenta, cerise, coral, tangerine and crimson. Tyres were the only indication that there was a bicycle frame hidden under the explosion of flowers.

After walking one and a half times round the lake, we sat on a bench and listened to the traffic gaining momentum until it reached a deafening drone. Bikes and mopeds and motorbikes and cars and trucks became a solid swaying mass. It moved like a stinking, wailing beast with no head or tail.

It took a long time to cross the road. Picking our way through lanes of traffic, we had to walk, stop, dodge, walk, swerve, pause, scamper. We found a café to have breakfast. You almost missed the doorway it was so small and overshadowed by its neighbours. It had patterned floor tiles, worn benches, and framed pictures of Uncle Ho marching with the soldiers. Mint green shutters were open to reveal the blackened cathedral opposite and the road below. We looked down at a pavement full of people on plastic stools, all crouching over steaming bowls of breakfast noodle soup. Next to them, a balding fleabag shook with the strain of a shit that wouldn't come easily. We watched women in conical hats forced into bandy-legged gaits under the weight of baskets of oranges.

On the curb over the street, an old woman flipped spitting eggs with chopsticks, keeping one eye on her son. He roamed up and down grunting, a child trapped in a flawed adult body. When the food was cooked, she moved him – obediently malleable – under a tree and placed the bowl in front of him. He squatted so low that his gnarly tailbone met the ground.

'That's a life sentence,' he said, under his breath. 'Looking after her son as if he's still a baby.'

I didn't comment. He probably thought I wasn't bothered, when really I found their relationship so terrifying I couldn't speak. Who would look after him when she was gone? The disabled man's patchy skin and open-mouthed gumming of white mush put me off my food. I continued to stare at the menu and each time the perky waitress came to take our order, I shook my head. On her fourth attempt I ordered.

When our drinks arrived, he spilled most of his fruit juice, then absentmindedly mopped it up in a well-practised way.

'So, what do you do at home?' I asked.

'Herpetologist,' he answered between mouthfuls of omelette.

'Herpes expert?'

'Reptile and amphibian expert. Doctor, actually.' He double-raised his eyebrows in a jokey way to show that I should be impressed.

'You don't look like an academic.'

'And academics look…?'

'Pasty. Skinny…or fat. Possibly ginger. Ill-fitting jumpers, bottle-top glasses, socks and sandals.'

'And how do *I* look?' he asked.

'Good. I mean, well…'

When I lifted my gaze from the table, his dimple was showing.

'Well, I'll take *that* as a compliment.'

'Although you do have egg in your beard, Doctor,' I added.

'Yep, saving that for later. Thanks.'

My attention kept being drawn to the brightly-inked propaganda posters above his head. The slogans were yelling at me:

Victory Will Definitely Be Ours.
Don't Let Them Escape.
Keep Your Belief Strong.

Lost and Found

Elizabeth Dawson

Prologue

Hello.

Can you hear me?

Probably not, the reception is terrible up here. Hang on; I don't know why I just said 'up', I'm not 'up' at all. It's more that I'm out – sideways – look, I'm just somewhere new, okay. It's weird but much nicer than I expected. Although I don't know what's coming next. Not that I'm picturing anything scary, I always said the living were the ones to worry about. Speaking of which, someone *down there* lied to me about ghosts and spooks. A right mess that got me into earlier today. Next thing I knew, I'd left my body and returned to eternal consciousness. It doesn't matter though because it turns out all of the things I've been worrying about – they were all just practice. I've got at least 103 more lifetimes to get them wrong again and learn more. Each time, I'll forget this place, which is a shame because it's phenomenally beautiful. It feels intensely violet, if you want to try and picture it. There's a sense of absolute completeness, of... purpose. And I don't mean that feeling you get when you've finished your shopping or your job for the day. It's so much more than that.

There are millions of other people here too but we don't take human form in this place. If you could perceive us without exploding, you'd see smears of astral dust bobbing around in, well, nothing. We're hanging around somewhere that looks like space, as though we're kids on a street corner but with less attitude and more cosmic stuff.

Have you ever thought that when you're looking at the night sky, maybe you're seeing something really obvious? Instead of trying to explain the universe, you should know it's just THEM reminding you what you are – it's a photograph of your origins if you like. No? Well, it's just a thought. Before I go, I just want to say, there are lots of people out there who will say they can contact the dead.

Some of them will charge you lots of money for it. But let me tell you no one up here can speak to us. If they did, their brains would burn inside their skulls. You don't need to worry about the people you love though, they're all moving in and out of the laundry machine, taking a spin, having a rest then diving back in. Just like you will. The important ones stick with you as well – you might not recognise them in this lifetime, or the next one, or the one after that, but you'll be around at the same time so you can find each other again and mess it all up. Or, maybe you'll be lucky.

Oh, I'm fading, so just quickly a shout out to Sergeant Brown, Duty Officer, Stoke Newington Police Station. The one who wouldn't let me drive the squad car and made jokes about women in handcuffs. THEY, by the way, THEY are a woman. Told you so.

Chapter One

It all started with a body on Holloway Road. Can you imagine how many other stories might have started that way? A snog in the dark, a knife in the back, a tango past a kebab shop. But no, this one was a murder – and it began on that filthy, gum-pocked shopping strip of a road in the middle of North London.

It was a cold morning, 7am, still dark and I hadn't had a cup of tea which was bad news for everyone. I had been N16's neighbourhood PC for three years and spent far too much of it giving talks in schools. In fact, I had one pencilled in for 8.30am that morning. That meant I had fifteen minutes to get into my uniform, five for a cup of tea, then half an hour at the computer printing off fact sheets about drug abuse and knife crime. You know, the usual teenage concerns.

I was fastening my belt when the duty sergeant stuck his head around the door.

'WPC Massam. Call for you. A homeless in Holloway Road. PC Thomas can drive.'

As we walked to the garage behind the station Pete told me more. A shopkeeper had called in to complain about a homeless outside his shop who wouldn't move. I daresay the shopkeeper didn't want to touch the sleeping bundle because why would you do that, when you could call a police officer to do your dirty work for you?

'Had your tea, grumpy?' said Pete as we got in the Astra. Sweet, steady, solid Pete – we did our probation together.

'No.'

'This won't take long. We can get breakfast after and I'll drop you at the school.'

'Good.'

We put the siren on and pegged it through traffic down to Holloway Road in 10 minutes. It wasn't strictly an emergency but the drive woke us up. I didn't say much and Pete knew me well enough not to push it. I just sat and stared at the trees and commuters whipping past the window, wondering what else the day would bring. There was that burglary down in Highbury, I'd promised to go and give the family some advice on security. Maybe *they'd* give me a cup of tea.

'AC News,' said Pete, nodding at the shop across the road from where he'd parked. In front, a black bin was concreted into the pavement. A male figure stretched out beside it, covered in blankets and a sprinkling of last night's chips. Only the face and feet were visible. We could both see he was dead before we'd got our seatbelts off. It was the stiffness in the body and the parchment colour of his skin. Still, as I held my hand up to stop the traffic and crossed the road, I hoped we were wrong.

It's amazing what people choose not to see. Pedestrians were striding past the bin, holding their coffees. Not one of them glanced at him. When I got close, I could see someone had thrown 10p at him. Before or after he died, I wondered, pulling on a pair of plastic gloves and stooping to check his pulse. There was no doubt about it, he was long gone. The man was aged around 40, blond, dirty hair, a few days of stubble, and well-fed for someone living on the streets, although he smelled rank. He was freezing cold to the touch and his mouth was stuck open, as it had been when he took his last breath.

'Can you do the honours Han?' said Pete.

I leaned forwards and closed the man's eyes. His eyelids felt cold and wrinkly under my fingertips, sliding over melon balls. Pete had to steel himself to touch dead people but it wasn't a problem for me. It was a duty, part of the responsibility we owed the dead once we took over their business. Poor bloke. I wondered who he'd been. As I started unwrapping the blankets to look for ID I heard a bell ringing and saw the owner of AC News stepping down onto the pavement.

'Hey, what's up with this guy?' he said.

'He's dead, sir,' I replied, standing up.

'What do you mean?' The shopkeeper came closer to look at the body then veered away, grimacing. 'I had no idea. I've only seen him through the glass. I come in the back way, you see. Christ, can you move him?'

'My colleague is calling an ambulance now sir,' I said, pointing at Pete, who was already on the radio. Then I bent back down to the body. There was something about the face that looked wrong but I couldn't work out what it was. The lips were blue, as you might expect from someone who'd died overnight in the freezing cold. Beneath his eyes there were lots of tiny, red pinpricks, the kind I'd seen before on people after they'd vomited a lot. The force of being sick bursts your blood vessels and the damage always shows under the eyes. It's the same as you see on bulimics.

'Pete, have you seen any sick nearby?'

'Sick? No. I don't want to find it either,' he said, checking the soles of his shoes.

I sighed and made a mental note to mention the red pinpricks in my notes. Meantime, the ambulance siren was getting closer. I stood up and took my gloves off, telling myself that I wasn't a detective, not yet anyway.

Once the ambulance had driven off, Pete went to the cafe across the road and got us two steaming cups of tea and a packet of custard creams each. It was fully light by then and we sat in the car drinking and eating the biscuits. Pete bit into his messily, as usual, and talked through the crumbs, dropping bits all over his trousers. Then he started laughing.

'That guy's still in his shop, watching us,' he said, nodding over the road. 'Bloody hell, you gave him the death stare. You should be nicer to people, you'll never find a boyfriend like that.'

'Pete, I wouldn't have HIM,' I said, waving my custard cream at him. 'He left a dead man outside his shop for hours, what a moron. Men are morons.'

'Hey, now, we're not all bad. How's it going with that Internet dating?'

'The last man I met told me he spent his spare time "playing the pink oboe". It was awful, I nearly arrested him.'

Pete half snorted and shook his head.

'I don't know why you're bothering – you could always go on a date with me?' he said, not looking me in the eye.

I turned and gave him my stern face for a good five seconds.

'No, Pete.'

'Why not?' he said, lightly.

I paused.

'You're too good looking.'

He paused.

'Well, yeah. Obviously.'

We both grinned and blew over the rims of our polystyrene cups. I liked that Pete was so fond of me. We both knew that when you've dealt with a dead body you feel freer than before. It's a temporary effect which makes you believe you can say or do anything you want for a few hours. In fact I was also thinking, while I finished my tea, that maybe later I'd go and have a chat with the murder squad about how that man had died. If it turned into something, they might ask me to help. Those little dots under his eyes, they were talking to me.

The Sky, The City, The Others

Sophie Playle

Ruth carried her daughter. She strained against the weight of the body balanced across her shoulder. The rifle, strapped to her bowed back, clacked as she walked. Her breath came out in bursts of hot clouds, crystallising in the air. The heaviness was compressing her joints and bones, slowly pushing her into the ground. But she mustn't give in – couldn't give in.

The narrow streets all looked the same. Cobbled pavements of black and grey, etched by heavy cart wheels and chipped by horse hooves. The iron streetlamps all looked the same, lined up like battered sentinels, some knocked to the ground, metal spines twisted and bent, glass heads smashed. The crumbling buildings all looked the same, pressed together, indistinguishable and looming. Narrow windows: broken, boarded up and dark. It was no use. She was lost.

With a roar, she allowed her knees to give way, her daughter sliding forwards into the cradle of her arms.

Hetti choked and gurgled, bubbles of spit and blood bursting at her lips. Her eyes were wide and rolled in her head, flashing white and bloodshot. 'Come on, Hetti, stay with me. Fight!' But Hetti's face was pale as smoke and her lips were tinged blue.

Though she felt so heavy, she looked so slight. A malnourished childhood meant she was small for her age, but she'd always been so strong. It broke Ruth's heart to see her so helpless and broken. She pulled the blanket tighter around her daughter's fragile body, the fabric now saturated with blood. It seeped through the thick weave and stained Ruth's hands.

She wiped at the tears that blotched her eyes and looked up and down the street. Squinting, she saw that a little further ahead, a faded sign protruded from above a shop window. It hung unevenly on its remaining hinge. In faded lettering it read: *Hathleheart's Apothecary*. Yes, that sounded familiar. She closed her eyes and saw herself approaching the shop, her long skirts brushing the pavement. She imagined the three huge glass bulbs that had sat in the window, pregnant with bright liquid – pink, teal, yellow – for the benefit of those who couldn't read. Her tinted reflections swelled as she approached. A bell tinkled as she pushed open the yellow door. Hathleheart spoke of new concoctions from the alchemist, as Ruth collected a vinegar, treacle and Laudanum remedy for Hetti, who was two years old at the time and suffering from a terrible cough.

Ruth pictured Doctor Hackley's surgery. She could see the building, solid, white-washed, with pillars either side of the door. Her mind flickered back to when she had last been inside the building, in its dark hallways and shadowed rooms. But she pushed that memory aside and instead tried to picture the route from the apothecary to the surgery. She had never walked it directly, but she pieced together a map in her head.

Hetti had become limp and quiet. Her lips were now bruised a deep blue and her eyes had closed. 'Hetti! Hetti!' Her head lolled on her shoulders as Ruth shook her. 'Wake up! Open your eyes! Come on now – stay with me!' She shook her again. 'Hetti!' Her throat tightened and the word broke in the air.

Hetti's eyes snapped open. She coughed, blood spattering Ruth's neck. She began to breathe again, slowly, laboured, rasping. Though her eyes remained open, they stared right through Ruth into nothingness.

They needed to keep moving. A loud crash echoed down an alley, like something metal had been dropped onto the pavement.

Ruth knotted the blanket tighter. She took a deep breath, pulled Hetti close and thrust her up over her shoulder once again. Clinging to her daughter with one arm, she used the other to help her stand. She cried out with exertion as she pulled herself to her feet.

A clearer path was now mapped in her head. She inhaled deeply, the rancid smell of the Thames sharp in her nose and throat. Boots heavy as she walked, she stepped through the debris of ruined market stalls, abandoned carts and broken furniture extracted from the guts of empty houses by scavengers.

Ruth turned down another street, relieved to see a familiar skyline: a jagged silhouette of descending rooftops, framed between two tall white buildings. Yes, yes, she recognised this place. To her right she could see the dark vein of the city's river. She turned left down Blackfriars Road, the street sign half eroded. A metallic scratching noise made her hairs stand on end and she turned to see a ragged parasol caught in the wind, skimming the pavement with its naked skeletal wires.

'Nearly there, girl. Just a little further.'

The Westside entrance to Nelson Square was in sight. Ruth's pulse throbbed in her ears. They were almost there – they'd almost made it. She just had to keep going. But when she turned the corner, she froze.

The sun was fading. The shadows of the heavy brick buildings were long and reaching. Ruth squinted, surveying the courtyard. There it was: Franklin's house. She was sure of it. It sat in the middle of the terraced houses, the opposite side of the square. The windows were boarded up, iron grates welded across them. About six feet from the front door slouched a dying bonfire.

Blood dripped from the soaked blanket rhythmically against the pavement. The distant flames sputtered, cracking damp wood like gunshot.

Another crash resonated somewhere behind them. It was hard to tell how far away it was. The network of streets, which had once been alive with the bustle and chatter of hundreds of people, were now empty echoing channels. Ruth surged forward. She could feel her energy waning, her muscles turning to lead. Her boot struck something hard and light, and it went skitting across the pavement. A skull.

She reached the door. It had once been a bright Colbert blue, but was now scorched by flames and encrusted with dirt. The wood had been shredded by the fingernails of frantic, clawing hands. Keeping one arm wrapped tightly around Hetti's legs, her bent body balanced on her shoulder, Ruth leaned against the door to keep them both upright. With her free hand, she pounded.

Each strike left a splattering of blood. 'Franklin! Franklin! Oh God, please, let us in! Franklin!'

Ruth struck the door again. In the distance, she heard the low rumble of animal groans. A long, laboured shriek – an aching, torturous sound – resonated, tapering into a croak, then silence. A clattering of wood – bodies clambering over debris. Ruth's heartbeat quickened and she felt faint with fear and exhaustion. The sounds almost didn't seem real, as though their threat was nothing more than a bad hallucination.

'Please. Franklin.' She wanted to shout, but the words came out in a dry whisper.

She had no idea if the doctor was still alive. It had been years since she was last here, though she was sure this was his property. The fire and fortified exterior suggested that the building was occupied. It could be anyone.

Ruth inhaled deeply. 'Let me in right now or I'll bring every one of these hellish creatures to your door!'

Behind her, something snarled. She snapped her head round. The clattering and wailing was growing louder, closer. At the two entrances to the square, she could just make out a scattering of figures in the shadows. Dull pinpricks of light reflected in a dozen pairs of distant, unblinking eyes. Though she knew the creatures were afraid of fire and of bright light, she felt exposed in the amber halo of the flames.

The sticky film of sweat coating Ruth's skin made her hair cling to her face like spilt ink. Her vision blurred and the world tilted. She hit the door with her fist one last time, then slid to the ground. There she hunched, Hetti again pulled into her lap. Blood spilled over her fingers as she pressed down with her remaining strength on Hetti's wound. On the stump of flesh where her lower arm used to be.

She had failed her daughter. Unable to protect her from the industrious machinery of the skies; unable to protect her from the violent terrors of the earth. In a way, it was a blessing that Hetti was only half conscious. That way the fear and the pain will be dulled when they come. It was Ruth's last thought before she collapsed into darkness.

But it wasn't darkness Ruth had fallen into. It was the hallway.

The door had opened, and Ruth and Hetti had fallen through. They landed next to two large boots that were connected to two long legs. Just before she passed out, Ruth looked up and saw the darkly sunken face of Doctor Hackley glaring down at her.

Selected Poems

Tracy Horn

Droplet leaves home

O
don't travel:
don't get in a car
a plane stay here where
the mild things are and say
thank god your head is bowed
that you eat little and work hard
and every day mark a little woe
that you didn't disobey me
and just go.

The open book on your knee

Of all the books
you could have taken from my
bookshelf: the Houllebecq swapped for
Harper Lee.
I wished I did not read the way I do.
I made a mental note to pull down
anything that might prompt
a paralysing cynicism in your
overview of this, our teeming world
(and hide it where?)
anything that might cause you to
look in a mirror and find your own
reflection wanting, anything that might
damn the seep from your core,
make tears that are literally
too salty for your eyes.
When you push back your
welter of curls and glower
at the twin torments: your sisters,
when you strike your baby brother
for good measure, toppling
nothing but mockery and laughter,
when you tilt your head toward the
glass and stare:
the pale fire of a city night fixes you there
serious and sad as all angels in prayer.

Mavis and Miles

The desks are scored into islands of five fours.
Mavis is telling me how her life was saved by Miles
Davis in that even if she didn't understand
how each note attached to the next
she was drawn to those who did

(She feels the same way about English
and the writer Martina Cole –
this is why she decided to enrol.)

That night locked in at the old Globe
Miles struck an altering chord of lust
she saw in the closed eyes of a quiet boy
something she could trust
she knew her first born would be
rocked in his arms and was not put off
that he couldn't speak her language
as the close dance where everything met
but their eyes, diminished the old anguish –
she says no one should stare too long
and too deep in the eyes of love
because what will you find there?
Stalking its hidden lair – a soul?
A halving of your hard won whole?

I'd rather not be blinded by doubt.
We stand – side by side – sketching out
our days – a coat sleeve on the arm of this child
a hat on the head of that, lost sock, found keys
or as night falls, so close we have only each other's
backs to watch if our eyes are open at all.

...Way too many to choose from... but
'In a Silent Way' or 'Kind of Blue'
the children were made to 'Bitches Brew'
and my sixteenths English mother-tongue
and their father's well-turned groove .

Demiurge

My god prefers
ontology to children
burning holes in their
water-wings down by the pool
(It's not his fault his dad was cruel)
Loves a camera, is charm and decency itself
to anyone in worsted, tweed, sudden wealth
My god is flaxen-haired, bullet-proof and nuclear in intent
My god dawns on me subtle as boredom every time I start to invent
My god is all life seen from every side – yet he himself – unverified
My god pulls every trigger, poisons every well
My god measures, cleaves, partakes and quells
My god tells me everything then says: never tell
hides flat feet and deep caesarean tread
underneath every second best bed
sleeps in dogs and children when weary
wakes up and walks with the dead.

About the Authors

The authors can be contacted through Ward Wood Publishing.

Helen Adie is a graduate of the Royal Holloway with a first in English and Drama. After working as an actress for 13 years she studied for a PGCE at Central and now teaches Drama and English at JAGS in Dulwich. Her poetry has appeared in publications including South Bank poetry magazine and Tramway's online literary magazine. Her poem 'They wear each other for disguise' was the winner of the 2010 Havant Poetry Prize. She is married to Simon Trewin and they have a teenage son, Jack. Helen is also a keen artist and her writing seeks to engage with the visual arts.

Timothy Allsop works as a writer and actor. He graduated from the Royal Holloway MA in Creative Fiction in 2010. He has published several short stories and was shortlisted in the Grist New Writing Competition and appears in their new anthology. He is currently writing a satire on the British education system called *Edify*. As an actor he has performed at the National and at Shakespeare's Globe and has played parts including Richard III, Thomas Becket and Oberon. He was born in East Anglia but currently lives in London and Shanghai.

Marion Ashton is a poet whose work has been published in several poetry magazines, including *The North, Mslexia* and *Smiths Knoll*. Formerly an English teacher, she now works part-time as an English advisor for a geological consultancy firm. Further information about Marion and more of her poems can be found on www.poetrypf.co.uk and www.arvonfoundation.org. The poem 'The Hide' was anthologised as 'The Hide at Minsmere' in *Glimmer*, Cinnamon Press, 2010. 'Modigliani and Spiders' Webs' appeared in *The Interpreter's House*, 2011. 'The Viewing' was published in *The North* Issue 44, November 2009. 'Before the Demolition' was published in *Dream Catcher* Issue 24, June 2011. 'At Abu Dhabi Airport' appeared in *Ambit,* Issue196, in 2009.

Annabel Banks is a prizewinning poet and fiction writer.
Learn more at annabelbanks.com
Contact: annabel.b@hotmail.com

J.K. Benecke grew up in Sweden and the UK, has an English degree from St Catharine's College, Cambridge, and has worked as a ghostwriter of film scripts in London and LA. *What Jack Did* is a novel told from two perspectives about regret, revenge, reading – and Sweden.

Mary Chamberlain is the author of popular and academic histories. *Fenwomen* - the first book to be published by Virago Press - *Old Wives' Tales*; *Growing Up In Lambeth; Narratives of Exile and Return; Family Love in the Diaspora: Migration and the Anglo-Caribbean Experience* and *Empire and nation-building in the Caribbean: Barbados 1937-1966*. Edited books include *Writing Lives*; *Caribbean Migration: Globalised Identities*; *Narrative and Genre*; *Caribbean Families in Britain and the Transatlantic World*; *Memories of Mass Repression*. She has lived and worked in England and the Caribbean and has served on a number of editorial and advisory panels, including Virago Press. She is currently working on a debut novel set in East Anglia in the 1930s. She is represented by Juliet Mushens at Peters, Fraser and Dunlop.

Kayo Chingonyi was born in Zambia in 1987 and came to the UK in 1993. He studied English Literature at The University of Sheffield where he completed an undergraduate dissertation on the work of Saul Williams and co-founded a live literature and music night called Word Life. His poems are published in *City Lighthouse* (Tall-Lighthouse, 2009), *The Shuffle Anthology* (Shuffle Press, 2009), *Verbalized* (British Council, 2010), *Paradise By Night* (Booth-Clibborn Editions 2010), *Clinic II* (Clinic Presents & Egg Box Publishing, 2011), *The Best British Poetry 2011* (Salt Publishing, 2011) and *The Salt Book of Younger Poets* (Salt Publishing, 2011). Chingonyi has performed his work across the UK at such venues and events as London Literature Festival, The Big Chill, Shakespeare's Globe, The RSC Swan Theatre, Tate Modern and Buckingham Palace and internationally at State Theatre of South Africa (Pretoria), New Space Theatre (Cape Town) and Museum Africa (Johannesburg).

He is a Visiting Writer at Kingston University and a pamphlet of his poems, entitled *Some Bright Elegance*, is due in 2012 from Salt Publishing.

Elizabeth Dawson used to write about alternative spirituality for a national women's magazine. This made her curious about concepts of the afterlife, what people believe and how we can be convinced of the seemingly impossible. These questions were the starting point for a novel about a young woman who gets tangled up with a psychic – the beginning of which is presented here. While at Royal Holloway Elizabeth also wrote a dissertation about the contemporary ghost story. Elizabeth studied history at Cambridge and finds inspiration in Norfolk.

Eamonn Doran was born in Dublin. He studied philosophy and French at NUI Maynooth and graduated in 2006 before studying for an MA in Creative Writing at the Royal Holloway, 2011. He has travelled extensively and currently lives between London and Dublin. *Eau de Vie* is an extract from a novel in progress.

Cecilia Ekback was born in Sweden in a northern fishing town. Her parents come from Lapland. During her adolescence in Sweden she worked as a journalist for the local newspaper and radio. At 15 she won a short story competition in one of Sweden's main newspapers. After university she specialised in marketing and worked for a multinational for fifteen years with postings in Russia, Germany, France, Portugal and the Middle East. She lives in London with her husband and two daughters, 'returning home' to the landscape and the characters of her childhood and adolescence in her writing. *Wolf Winter* is her first novel.
Contact: Karincecilia1@gmail.com

April Estrada was born in 1984 in San Diego, California, and holds a BA in English from Northern Arizona University and an MA in Creative Writing from Royal Holloway, University of London. She is currently working on a book-length series of poems and aims to begin pursuing a PhD in Creative Writing.

Jenni Fagan is the author of two poetry collections *Urchin Belle*, and *The Dead Queen of Bohemia* which won 3:AM Poetry Book of the Year. Her debut novel *The Panopticon* will be published by Random House in May 2012. She is currently living in Edinburgh with her newborn, and completing her next novel. For further enquiries please contact Tracy Bohan at the Wylie Agency.

William Fowler lives in west London and currently works as an advertising copywriter. This is the opening of a book, which will be a novel in two parts.

David Gill is from Cardiff, lives in Hackney and works in Brixton with vulnerable people. He has had short stories performed at the Liars' League, Storytails and Foyles and publications include The London Magazine, Interzone, Margin, The New Welsh Review, Planet, Tales Of The Decongested, The Frogmore Papers and Litro. He is about to start training to teach Physics at secondary schools in London.

Nora Gombos currently lives in Brighton. She worked as an actress and journalist in Oslo and London before starting her MA in Creative Writing at Royal Holloway. She won the 2011 Margaret Hewson Prize for her novel-in-progress, provisionally entitled *Pitchpoled*, and is also writing a children's book. The extract is from her novel. Contact: noragombos@gmail.com

Viv Graveson, a former news reporter and feature writer, now teaches Philosophy of Religion part-time at an independent school in St Albans. She has also taught English and has an MA in Psychoanalytic Psychology. She has written one other novel, *Threads*, and is married with a grown up son.

Kristina Heaney writes character-based fiction laced with trademark black humour. This excerpt is taken from her novel in progress *Ava Gates*, which has formed the backbone of her Creative Writing MA. She lives in north-west London, the setting for most of her writing. Visit her website at www.kristinaheaney.com

Tracy Horn is an English lecturer in Further Education and a poet. She was Born in 1961, and raised in Johannesburg, Margate and London.

Anna Kirk grew up in Northumberland before travelling south to study English Literature at UCL. She has lived, worked and studied in London for the past four years, regularly attending poetry readings and events across the city, and occasionally reading at them.

Rebecca Mackenzie grew up in Thailand, Malaysia and India. She worked for several years as a strategic planner in advertising, winning international awards for her campaigns. Rebecca now works as a writer and theatre maker and recently completed a year-long post as Artist in Residence at a central London church. The excerpt is from her first novel set amongst missionaries in China.

Laura McClelland was born in 1985 and grew up in Yorkshire. She completed her BA in Philosophy and English at the University of Cambridge in 2004. She is currently completing work on her novel about a group of Pre-Raphaelites, including Willam Morris and Dante Gabriel Rossetti. An extract from this novel won the inaugural Margaret Hewson prize, judged by the late Beryl Bainbridge and Johnson and Alcock literary agency, who awarded the prize. She lives in East Sussex.

Rosie Miller writes about the rural and urban working classes of her native county of Essex, and their frustrated journeys through salt marshes, dormitory towns and the outskirts of London. She is also writing a fictionalised memoir called *The Conscientious Objector*, about the widow of a 1930s poet with whom she lived whilst studying for her degree in English at University College London. Contact: rosemariecharlotte@googlemail.com

Carl Newbrook was born in South Shields and lives in London. He read English Literature and completed a D Phil at Oxford University and has worked in bookselling and publishing. He is currently completing a book of linked short stories.

Barney Norris's award-winning first play, *At First Sight*, was produced on tour and published in the spring of 2011. He works for the theatre company Out of Joint, is co-Artistic Director of Up In Arms, and is currently under commission writing a play for the Bush Theatre. He has also published poetry in several little magazines.

Thomas Ogier is London born, with New Zealand and Trinidadian blood, and he grew up on the island of Guernsey. He worked as a journalist, travelled, and studied English and Film at the University of Kent, before starting his MA at Royal Holloway. WAKE is his first attempt to write a novel. He is 26.

Diriye Osman is a Somali-born, British writer and artist. His fiction and non-fiction has been published by *Kwani?*, *Time Out* and *Fused*. He has two stories in the November 2011 issues of *Prospect* and *Attitude*. *The Telegraph* wrote of his work, 'My excitement over Osman and his writing comes, in part, out of delight at the impossibility of categorisation.' Osman is the deputy editor of *Scarf* Magazine, a cross-cultural arts publication, and is currently working on a collection of stories about gay and lesbian Somalis living in Nairobi and London.

Rebecca Perl spent five years in Munich working as an in-house writer and editor for magazines. Since returning to London in 2007, she has worked in higher education communications and continues to take freelance writing commissions. She is currently writing her first novel, a semi-autobiographical tale set in Middlesbrough and Czechoslovakia. Visit her website at www.rebeccaperl.co.uk

L.E. Peters read English at Emmanuel College, Cambridge and currently lives in London.

Rachel Piercey read English Literature at St Hugh's College, Oxford, where she was President of the Oxford University Poetry Society and won the Newdigate Prize in 2008. She went on to become a travel guide editor, before returning to university in 2010 to take her MA in Creative Writing.

Sophie Playle studied at UEA and worked in editorial publishing before embarking on the Creative Writing MA at the Royal Holloway. She is currently writing her first novel, an apocalyptic steampunk horror, which draws upon the research she undertook for her dissertation on the conflict and representation of the natural and the mechanical in steampunk fiction. Her short stories and poetry have appeared in various publications, such as: *The London Magazine*, *Friction Magazine*, *Every Day Fiction* and the *Hint Fiction Anthology*. She blogs regularly about writing and publishing at www.sophieplayle.com

Nigel Pollitt worked for many years as a writer and sub-editor on magazines and newspapers including *The Leveller*, *City Limits*, *Roof*, *The Observer* and *The Independent* before starting the MA. Poems in this selection have appeared in *Magma* and *South Bank Poetry*. His work also appears in *Smiths Knoll*. Nigel lives in north-east London. The poems 'Tulips' and 'New World' were published in *Magma*. 'Northern Line, Angel to King's Cross' appeared in *South Bank Poetry*.

Saskia Sarginson studied Fashion at St Martin's School of Art and later read English Literature at Cambridge. Saskia was Health & Beauty Editor of *Company*, then worked as a script reader and freelance journalist (*Zest*, *Cosmopolitan*, *Sunday Times*, *You* magazine and others). She's a ghost writer for, among others, Harper Collins and the BBC. She has other non-fiction books published by Ebury Press, and a short story in *The Lounge Companion Vol.2*. Saskia has taught for the charity The Kids Company; she also dances tango and teaches English Literature. She lives in London with her partner, four children and various animals. She's working on her novel, *No Long Way Round*. Her agent is Eve White.

Sally Skinner was born in Derbyshire in 1981. She studied English at Girton College, Cambridge and works as a freelance writer and ad creative. 'Man, Walking' is an extract from her first novel, provisionally titled *The Fleeting*.

Hilary Standing trained as an anthropologist and social scientist. She has been a teacher and researcher at the University of Sussex and a Fellow of the Institute of Development Studies. She is now an Emeritus Professor. She has had a lifelong professional and personal interest in international development and its dilemmas and has lived and worked for many years in India and Bangladesh. The idea of writing fiction focused on these dilemmas came several years ago and led to the decision to embark on a Creative Writing MA. She is working on her first novel, *The Inheritance Powder*, which is excerpted here. Contact: hilarystanding@yahoo.co.uk

Lyn Thornton has a degree from Oxford University in English. She graduated in 1979. After a career in publishing in London she returned to Oxford to tutor in English literature.
Contact: lynthornton@btinternet.com

James Trevelyan was born in 1988 and grew up in the Midlands. He studied English and Creative Writing at Lancaster University and now lives in South London.

Lauren Trimble was born in Dallas, Texas. She taught English in Japan before moving to London where she now works for Bloomsbury publishing. She is currently writing a novel about a Baptist minister and his wife Beth Anne, who has severe frontal lobe brain damage.

Katy Tucker grew up on the Isle of Man among tailless cats and fairies. Consequently, she is interested in the effects isolation has on consciousness, and the ways in which storytelling can be used to express one's perception of the world. In 2008, she founded the online magazine Frameus, a repository for Manx artists to publish poetry, short fiction, serialisations, articles, scripts and digital artwork. Katy also co-edited the fiction magazine Route 57, wrote for BBC Isle of Man, and has published several short stories, poems and articles. Katy writes and performs comedy stage shows, both solo and as a group, and has just completed a festival circuit with the show 'Four Women, Nine Tits.'

Christian Ward is a 31-year-old London-based poet who completed the MA in Creative Writing at Royal Holloway, University of London, in November 2010. His work has appeared in journals such as *Iota*, *Poetry Wales* and *The Warwick Review*. He won the 2010 East Riding Open Poetry Competition and was shortlisted for the 2010 Bridport Prize and Arvon International Poetry Competition. His first collection, *The Moth House*, is due for release in spring 2012 from Scarborough-based Valley Press. 'The Real Red Riding Hood' won 1st prize in the SLQ (April 2010) Poetry Competition; 'Girl on the District Line' won 1st prize in the 2010 East Riding Open Poetry Competition; 'Teleshopping' was previously published in *Iota*; 'Filming "The Beheading of Daniel Pearl"' won 1st prize in the 2010 Sentinel Literary Festival Poetry Competition; 'Spock' won 3rd prize in the SLQ (Oct 2010) Poetry Competition; 'The Butterflies, Kew Gardens' was short listed in the 2010 Arvon International Poetry Competition.

Georgina Wolfe is a practising barrister. She read English Literature at Edinburgh University before going to law school in London. She was called to the Bar by Middle Temple in 2006 and was a Queen Mother Scholar and a Harold G Fox Scholar. Georgina co-authored a non-fiction guide to becoming a barrister *The Path to Pupillage* which is now in its second edition (Sweet & Maxwell, 2008). Georgina writes short stories and is currently working on her first novel set in 1970s Switzerland. She lives in London.

Alphabetical Listing of Authors

Adie, Helen	Selected Poems	**50**, 219
Allsop, Timothy	Edify	**81**, 219
Ashton, Marion	Selected Poems	**136**, 219
Banks, Annabel	Faringdon Park	**86**, 220
Benecke, J.K.	What Jack Did	**59**, 220
Chamberlain, Mary	The Excursion	**168**, 220
Chingonyi, Kayo	Selected Poems	**29**, 220
Dawson, Elizabeth	Lost and Found	**206**, 221
Doran, Eamonn	*Eau de Vie*	**35**, 221
Ekback, Cecilia	Wolf Winter	**45**, 221
Estrada, April	Selected Poems	**9**, 221
Fagan, Jenni	Porcelain Sunflower Seeds	**131**, 222
Fowler, William	Time Death	**103**, 222
Gill, David	The Lives of the Saints	**98**, 222
Gombos, Nora	Pitchpoled	**15**, 222
Graveson, Viv	Silence & Shadows	**184**, 222
Heaney, Kristina	Ava Gates	**152**, 222
Horn, Tracy	Selected Poems	**215**, 223
Kirk, Anna	Selected Poems	**173**, 223
McClelland, Laura	The Strawberry Thief	**179**, 223
Mackenzie, Rebecca	Aboard a White Ship	**65**, 223
Miller, Rosie	The Tulip	**125**, 223
Newbrook, Carl	Abundance	**142**, 223
Norris, Barney	Longing	**190**, 224
Ogier, Thomas	Disappear Here	**107**, 224
Osman, Diriye	Ndambi	**24**, 224
Perl, Rebecca	Keep Your Belief Strong	**201**, 224
Peters, L.E.	The Chinese Room	**76**, 224
Piercey, Rachel	Selected Poems	**157**, 224
Playle, Sophie	The City, The Sky, The Others	**211**, 225
Pollitt, Nigel	Selected Poems	**114**, 225
Sarginson, Saskia	No Long Way Round	**147**, 225
Skinner, Sally	Man, Walking	**40**, 225
Standing, Hilary	The Inheritance Powder	**19**, 226
Thornton, Lyn	Selected Poems	**194**, 226
Trevelyan, James	Selected Poems	**70**, 226
Trimble, Lauren	Southwest Twizzle	**120**, 226
Tucker, Katy	A Darkness in the Bones	**163**, 226
Ward, Christian	Selected Poems	**92**, 227
Wolfe, Georgina	*Étienne*	**55**, 227

Copyright Holders

Selected Poems © April Estrada 2011
Pitchpoled © Nora Gombos 2011
The Inheritance Powder © Hilary Standing 2011
Ndambi © Diriye Osman 2011
Selected Poems © Kayo Chingonyi 2011
Eau de Vie © Eamonn Doran 2011
Man, Walking © Sally Skinner 2011
Wolf Winter © Cecilia Ekback 2011
Selected Poems © Helen Adie 2011
Étienne © Georgina Wolfe 2011
What Jack Did © J.K. Benecke 2011
Aboard a White Ship © Rebecca Mackenzie 2011
Selected Poems © James Trevelyan 2011
The Chinese Room © L.E. Peters 2011
Edify © Timothy Allsop 2011
Faringdon Park © Annabel Banks 2011
Selected Poems © Christian Ward 2011
The Lives of the Saints © David Gill 2011
Time Death © William Fowler 2011
Disappear Here © Thomas Ogier 2011
Selected Poems © Nigel Pollitt 2011
Southwest Twizzle © Lauren Trimble 2011
The Tulip © Rosie Miller 2011
Porcelain Sunflower Seeds © Jenni Fagan 2011
Selected Poems © Marion Ashton 2011
Abundance © Carl Newbrook 2011
No Long Way Round © Saskia Sarginson 2011
Ava Gates © Kristina Heaney 2011
Selected Poems © Rachel Piercey 2011
A Darkness in the Bones © Katy Tucker 2011
The Excursion © Mary Chamberlain 2011
Selected Poems © Anna Kirk 2011
The Strawberry Thief © Laura McClelland 2011
Silence & Shadows © Viv Graveson 2011
Longing © Barney Norris 2011
Selected Poems © Lyn Thornton 2011
Keep Your Belief Strong © Rebecca Perl 2011
Lost and Found © Elizabeth Dawson 2011
The City, The Sky, The Others © Sophie Playle 2011
Selected Poems © Tracy Horn 2011